OBSIDIAN MURDER

A Violet Carlyle Mystery

BETH BYERS

SUMMARY

Bonfire Night 1924.

Violet, Victor, and friends intend to celebrate an evening with cocktails, bonfires, and fireworks. What they don't intend is to find a body instead of their Guy Fawkes. What's even more baffling? The obsidian blade. Once again, the friends delve into a wicked crime. Tensions rise as they realize that murder wasn't the only game afoot during the celebration.

CHAPTER ONE

"What's all this?" Lila demanded as Violet made her way into the house.

Vi shoved her multitude of bags and hat boxes behind her back and shrugged innocently.

"There's too many for that, my girl," Lila told Vi with a smirk. "Someone felt the need to buy everything from the shops today?"

Vi had hoped to escape a witness to the madness. The problem was that Violet should have had her purchases delivered to her house rather than appearing with the evidence in hand. Or rather, her real problem was that her old grey days had appeared that morning with a sense of needing to do something to allay those blues before her brother or Jack returned and found her curled up in her bed with her hair in a mess and her skin turned sallow.

Her stupid, lascivious brother had married and gone to Paris without her. It was his honeymoon, so she only blamed him partially. If Victor and Kate hadn't needed to be married

1

posthaste due to an impending bundle of joy, Violet would have prepared a way to distract herself while they were gone. Instead, they'd left suddenly and Violet had been forced to recognize just how horribly dependent she was on her brother.

It was a fact she hated. They hadn't spent more than a few days apart since Victor had left for the war. He hadn't ended up serving in battle because he'd been injured in training and then the war ended before he healed. Back then, Violet had known what to do. She'd volunteered in the efforts, helped as was needed, and done what could be done from the Homefront, praying the whole time her brother would return to her. She knew it had been a close thing—she had, after all, lost two older brothers to the war.

"My life," she told Lila seriously, "is too wrapped up in my twin."

"You two are rather dependent on each other. It would help having Victor gone if Jack hadn't had to go catch murderers so far away."

"I feel like a failure," Vi told Lila. "Am I not a modern woman? I don't need Jack here. I need...something else."

Lila scoffed and then took Violet's bags from her, setting them down in the center of the entry hall to grab Vi by the arm. "Tea, Hargreaves," Lila told the butler waiting at hand, "and some frivolous and ridiculous treat, if available."

He nodded and lifted several of Violet's purchases, disappearing into the house while Lila dragged Violet into the parlor.

"Being modern doesn't mean not loving someone." Lila sounded a little like one of their instructors.

Violet scrunched up her nose and threw herself onto the Chesterfield near the fire, dropping her arm over her eyes so she didn't have to see Lila's knowing gaze. The woman wouldn't, however, let Violet moan in peace.

"You tend towards the blues and greys, my darling. You went out to make sure you didn't end up in a tangle of limbs and hair by the time your boys came home, didn't you?"

Violet nodded with her arm over her eyes.

"It's perfectly acceptable to love someone. It's perfectly acceptable to have the blues. My brother spends the entirety of every winter seeing the worst of everything. Then, lo and behold, the sun comes back, and he goes wandering the woods again without being soaked through, and he's a different creature. It happens, darling. Good for you in escaping into shopping rather than moping."

Violet raised her arm to scowl at Lila and then dropped it back down. She was having one of those moments where she knew she should strap on a cheery face and drop a joke, but she didn't want to. Violet didn't have to pretend for Lila, who was her oldest friend. They'd gone to the same boarding school and college and shared a room for much of that time. Lila could and had taken the worst of Violet.

"Have you heard? There was a fire at that new little museum off of Hyde Park."

"What, no? Why do you know?" Violet lifted her head enough to examine Lila. "Why do you even care?"

"Denny's brother was there when the fire started. Everyone got out, but he said it was quite a close thing. He just showed up at our door, sooty and wild-eyed, requesting a bath and a suit. Turns out it's the third fire his patron has had started at his properties!"

She knew she should care more than she did, but Violet was having a hard time amassing concern. She dropped her head back to the Chesterfield. "A house fire is a good idea for a book. Jane Eyre-style perhaps, with someone saved at the last minute. He's fine?"

"A bit of a cough and swimming in Denny's suit. It's hard to believe that Denny used to be svelte. He's so rotund now. A bit of a porker. Little brother is so slim. Maybe you should kill someone in your new book? Someone porky who cannot adequately run from danger. I'll give Denny the rest of the message."

"Does he really read our books?" Violet asked with disinterest, finding she didn't care all that much.

"He does. I would mind far less if he didn't read them with a bottle of wine and a box of chocolates, giddy like a child to see what madness you two have concocted."

Violet smiled at the image Lila presented before she curled onto her side, propped her head on her hand and admitted, "I don't feel like writing." Violet hated being blue. *Hated* it. More, she hated feeling as though the reason she was blue was because her brother was away enjoying his first weeks with his bride and Jack was away working. She was *not* a dependent creature.

"Maybe you should go bother your man of business and buy something ridiculous. A company? Oooh! A confectioner's shop? Finance a fashion career? Buy something from ancient Rome?"

Violet grunted.

"Let's go visit Ginny," Lila suggested. "She's at school suffering. She needs her guardian to appear with treats."

Violet shook her head still propped on her arm. "She's just settling in. I think if we appeared, it would be entirely unwelcome."

"Do they still call her Lady Guttersnipe?"

"She's decided to channel a lofty disposition when it comes to such shenanigans."

"Ah," Lila said. Vi could hear her friend rustle but didn't bother to get up. The door to the parlor opened, and a tea cart was rolled across the floor. There was more rustling, and then Lila nudged Vi with her shoe. "Sit up, darling. Drink this tea. It's almost entirely whiskey."

Violet sniffed and sat fully up, taking the tea with a scowl.

"Don't look at me like that, my girl. I'm not the one who snuck about with Kate and didn't learn about modern *prevention* methods."

"But then," Violet said after a long sip of tea that left her nose burning, "a Violet junior wouldn't be on the way."

"Too true," Lila said with a grin. "How many of those bags were full of baby things?"

Violet shrugged. The answer was rather a lot. She had also, however, found a new kimono with silver and purple dragons and a delightful nude day dress that drew attention to Violet's slenderness.

"Cheer up, love," Lila ordered as she handed Violet a plate of petit fours. "This is just a grey day. Nothing to pummel yourself over."

"I feel a little—"

"Do you think I don't know what it's like? I was quite despondent the last time Denny went off with his brother for one of his masculine weekends of pints and whatever else they do. I suspect they simply drink the whole time. I quite scolded myself raw over it."

"I do hate that I feel so blue when I should be happy for Victor."

"You aren't grieving that he married Kate," Lila told Violet flatly. "You're worrying in advance that you won't know what to do without him around daily."

Violet winced.

"Especially because you *want* to be married to Jack and *want* Victor to be married to Kate. You simply have forgotten how to be apart from your twin, and it doesn't help that he's rather the

BETH BYERS

most ideal of brothers or that you two have done everything together for so long neither of you know how to do without the other. Victor uses you to manage his household and finances and to defend him from your grasping relatives. You use him to manage your tendency towards the blues. Neither of you write as well without the other."

Violet flinched.

"Time to redefine yourself, my love. Shall we look into one of those ladies' clubs or start up an orphanage? Become the patron of an artist? You aren't the only one at loose ends. Denny suggested that we have a child since Victor and Kate were. I—I don't know if I'm suited to motherhood."

Violet put down her teacup and realized all of the sudden that Lila hadn't appeared only to help Violet but to seek help for herself. Suddenly her blues started to fade. "Do you want my honest opinion?"

Lila bit her lip, her gaze darting to the side, and Violet winced —internally this time—for Lila. Vi waited, letting her friend have all the time she needed.

"Yes."

"Honestly, darling? You're already a mother, my love. You have been taking care of Denny for so long that you don't realize that you have the skills and all the ability to sacrifice. And do not discount your fiendish sister. How often do you go home and step in for your parents? The little ones will be easier than your Martha or Denny. And now that Denny inherited, you can hire someone to change the nappies."

Lila's mouth twisted. It was her turn to grunt in reply and sip her loaded tea to avoid answering.

"I think you'd be a good mother," Violet said, leaning down so Lila had to meet Vi's gaze and see the honesty there.

"What about you and Jack?"

"And babies?" Violet shook her head. "I—oh."

Lila laughed and then demanded, "Can you believe Denny asked about children? He says to me yesterday over dinner, 'What about it, my love? Shall we procreate and fill the world with chubby younglings?'"

Violet could hear Denny's lazy voice asking in just that way, and she shook her head. "What did you say?"

"I couldn't speak," Lila replied dryly. "I was too busy choking on the soup."

Violet laughed and the last of her blues faded. She leaned back, crossed her legs, and asked, "Am I weak?"

"It's perfectly acceptable to love someone and miss them," Lila replied. "That's what my mother told me when it was me in this boat."

Violet nodded and scolded herself once again. This time, however, she felt brighter about it. Things were fine. She would find balance again without daily Victor. It wasn't like she hadn't lived that way previously. A new balance, a new life, a new partnership—they'd always be twins.

"Cocktails tonight, my love," Lila declared. "While I debate Denny's plans for a family, I need to indulge my bright young thing. Stay up late, dance without a care, enjoy my svelte form."

"You are not a—ah—wife who has to change everything with a child, my love," Violet told Lila seriously. "You are rather spoiled."

"Yes, but I suspect I'll be one of those cooing mothers who talks about their infant all of the time while others look on in boredom and consider whether they should acquire new friends."

"I shall stay reliable, especially if you name this child Violet junior."

Violet set aside her doctored tea and plate of petit fours and rummaged through the cart, looking for a sandwich, and discovered a coffee pot behind the teapot. Oh, the lovely Hargreaves who anticipated Violet's wants so easily. She poured herself a cup of Turkish coffee and then placed a cucumber sandwich on her plate. Violet did love cucumbers and the mix of butter and herbs.

"Look, you're feeling better," Lila said. "Victory is mine!"

CHAPTER TWO

"You're sneakier than I thought," Violet told her twin as she stretched her toes towards the ceiling the next afternoon. She felt like she'd tangled with a black cab the previous evening and ended very much the loser. Waking had been vicious when her own groan had been the noise that jerked her awake. Violet had shoved her eye mask back, glanced blearily around her room, dug out a couple of aspirin, downed them and curled back onto her side.

She'd fallen back to sleep the moment she decided to remain abed for the day. To be fair, she hadn't thought Victor and Kate were returning that day. He'd arrived in Violet's room, thrown himself on her bed, and sent her bouncing into the air, waking her for the second time.

"I don't know what you're talking about," Victor lied.

"Ah, brother," Violet groaned. "You know exactly to what I refer. Having to get married in a rush. I never did see signs of shenanigans between you two, and to be honest, I'm surprised. I know everything about you."

"Except that."

"I probably shouldn't know that," she mused, examining her pajamas. Perhaps she would have dressed for the day if she had realized Victor and Kate were returning to London. Surely they had intended to stay longer? Violet thought they had intended more time in Paris, but she wasn't quite sure of the date. Why had they come back? Did Victor somehow know she was drowning in the blues?

Maybe she was wrong about the length of the stay in Paris? Violet couldn't count on anything that required her wits given how the space behind her eyes ached. Her stomach was roiling. With Giles and his magical concoctions unavailable, she'd been forced to suffer through the morning.

It all came back to Lila and Denny. Lila wanted to keep Violet cheery and dragged her out for cocktails and dancing. Too many cocktails in fact. Too late of a night, in fact. With far too spicy Indian food sometime after midnight.

"Shall I call you Papa Bear now? Daddy-O? Sneaky, sneaky Daddy-O?"

Victor blushed lightly. "It wasn't like...ahh...leave it. You're a vixen. You should be focused on spoiling the kid and not bedeviling me."

Violet laughed as Victor scowled. "Time to grow up, my little flower. Being the Daddy-O is a serious business. I purchased rather a ridiculous amount of things for the little mite while you were gone."

"What am I going to do? By Jove, Vi! I'm not ready to be a parent," Victor moaned. "The only skill I have is making cocktails. It turns out that's frowned upon for children. My goodness, I don't know that I've ever held a baby, and Kate says I must hold ours."

Violet's laugh had their two spaniels lifting up their heads to examine their people before shooting them both a look that was very much a command to silence.

"Don't laugh," Victor whined.

"It's funny," Violet told him without a smidgeon of apology. "Daddy. Papa." Violet's laughter increased with each dramatic wince. Marrying Kate was everything Victor had ever wanted— becoming a father terrified her twin into his wits leaving.

"Oh, is it?" Victor's gaze narrowed on hers, and his eyes filled with a wicked joy. "Did you know Father took Jack and Tomas shooting before we left the homestead?"

There was too much glee in that question for Violet to feel comfortable. "Ah, no."

"Seems their guns were malfunctioning, so only Father had a rifle that worked." Victor's laugh was an evil cackle. "Father explained it was one thing for a son to have to marry quickly. He'd hate to see the same thing for his daughters."

"Ahh," Violet choked, sitting fully upright and staring at her twin. His dark eyes and sharp features were enjoying her blush far too much. "No." The last bit was a plea, but her prayer was too late.

"He expects to walk his daughters down the aisle as slim and beautiful on their wedding day as they were the morning of this conversation."

"What now?" Violet bit her bottom lip until it hurt just to see if this were real and not actually some sort of hallucination.

"It gets better," Victor added gleefully. "You know how good Father is with a gun. He spent the entire time talking to them about *respecting* his daughters while shooting a fly off of a leaf or some other such madness."

Violet flopped back onto her bed, put her arm over her face, and groaned. Victor's chuckle was a terrible echo of her laughter when he and Kate were pushed into an early wedding for their approaching bundle of joy. Violet was excited to be an aunt, but she had been more excited at the time to watch Victor's face flush a brilliant red as he'd told her why they were marrying so quickly.

She had, of course, guessed by that point, but she'd made him lay it all out, playing stupid while his betrothed had choked back her laughter. Vi should have known that Kate would eventually explain that Violet had guessed, and he would get revenge. He always did.

She knew it when she'd played her games with him, but as twins, they were two sides of the same coin, and not just because they looked alike. They both took after their mother: tall, slender, with sharp features, dark coloring, and cleverness in their air. More than that, however, they understood each other completely and thought similarly.

"Did Father tell you of this momentous occasion or was it Jack?"

"I saw them come in from their little adventure. Jack seemed like he'd gone for a stroll through the roses. Entirely unruffled. I can assure you I was not so comfortable when I had to walk with Kate's father before the wedding. Tomas, however, looked as though he were about to expire on the spot. I suspect that he may have...ah...previously...engaged...you know what I mean."

"No need to elaborate," Violet told her twin. She didn't want to know about her little sister's passions. "So Tomas was the one who spilled about their little interlude with Father?"

"Indeed," Victor replied, and they shuddered in unison. He'd already faced the music as far as Kate went, and she was his wife now. Violet was almost positive that Victor could hardly believe his luck. He seemed to spend random moments gazing into the distance in a surreal haze, shocked that his dreams had come true.

Violet sat back up. Jack hadn't reacted to her father in any way as far as Vi could tell. Her mind was skipping over the last few weeks, trying to recall. She doubted her father wanted to push Jack away, so perhaps Jack hadn't been too bothered? He hadn't been behaving differently since they'd finally announced their engagement. She considered how he did act, and any dawning worries were slain before they could take flight. Jack loved her, and he showed it with his actions.

"I've hired an assistant to plan the wedding with Beatrice as a main go-between. I've discovered I have little desire to do more than select my dress and the date," Violet told Victor. "I think we should consider a month by the sea somewhere. Perhaps even somewhere warmer."

Victor's head cocked as he considered. "Is it time yet to go back to the Amalfi coast? It has been a while. I confess I'd like to escape such easy access on the part of Kate's mother. She's driving me mad."

Violet smirked. Mrs. Lancaster was finding a good number of reasons to come to London. She'd already planned two trips, and each of those seemed to require that she spend a day or two with her daughter. Violet could understand Mrs. Lancaster's desire to visit with her daughter, but she'd also used the opportunity to school Victor. If he didn't escape again soon, he and Kate wouldn't be able to without Mrs. Lancaster including herself in the plans.

"I suppose we have to start asking Jack and Kate where they want to go," Violet sighed, but her tone was light and teasing and Victor grinned in reply.

Victor crossed his legs. "I believe in marrying Kate, I have somehow bequeathed my vote to her. Jack, however, will never get a vote. It'll always be yours."

"Am I such a dragon?" She dropped back to her bed and crossed her arms behind her head. "I've been thinking we should write a series of detective stories where the culprits are monsters.

The first monster should, of course, be Lady Eleanor with fangs and claws. Perhaps one of the detectives will have a small child."

"A child?"

"A girl."

"Perhaps a Vi Junior?" Victor guessed.

"Perhaps," Violet mused. "After all, you'll know about being a parent soon. Since the horrendous Miss Allen revealed our *actual* names, Mr. Monroe from the publishing company states we should start publishing under Lady Vi and her lesser brother."

Victor groaned at Vi's joke. An article had been published revealing the twins as the author V.V. Twinnings and stated that Victor was the lesser twin.

"We've already decided upon names for the little mite."

"Have you then?" Violet waited with her brows lifted, and even though he couldn't see her face with her flopped back, he knew her well enough to guess at her expression.

"Peter Lionel if we have a boy."

Naming a boy after the brothers they'd lost in the Great War was almost painful.

Violet nodded at Victor to prevent herself from thinking too hard about their lost brothers. With her dreams lately, the last thing Vi needed was to spend time thinking about the dead. Better to focus on the good.

"And Vi Junior if it's a girl?"

"We were considering either Agatha or after Mama and call her Penelope name. I suggested we put them both together and do Agatha Penelope, but Kate reminded me that we may well have more than one girl." There was just enough of a tremble in Victor's voice for Violet to be able to laugh even though her heart was in her throat. Was she ready to love another Agatha? Losing Aunt Agatha had been painful indeed, and to have a near-daily reminding of their loss would be difficult. Violet wasn't sure she could do it, but she was also sure that no one deserved to be memorialized with a name more than Aunt Agatha.

Violet smiled at the thought of a little Agatha and then blinked the shine in her eyes away before her twin sat up and noticed. She curled onto her side and then rolled off the bed. "Out with you. I've decided to get dressed today after all. Where is my love, Kate?"

"She went to wash up and I suspect curled up on her bed. She's been falling asleep at the drop of a hat. If she didn't have a maid keeping an eye on her in the bath, she might just drown."

Violet smacked her brother's foot and ordered him from the room. A near-drowning in the bath seemed like just the thing to start this—ah—afternoon out correctly.

It was coming up on Bonfire Night in a day or two—she really should look up the date—and a chilly rain had settled on London with a vengeance. She could hear the splatter of raindrops on the window panes, and the bath she'd lingered in warmed the portion of her bones she hadn't realized had become quite so cold. Looking back, she should have brought a coat with her the previous evening instead of just her wrap. Without Jack to wrap an arm around her shoulders, she'd become thoroughly chilled.

Violet slowly dressed in front of her fire. There was very little about the day that demanded she hurry. She thought she'd have some tea and then return to her bedroom to start the new book. She hadn't realized how much she needed Victor to bounce ideas off of. Normally, when they wrote, she started the story and he read after her, leaving notes, and then carried on from where she left off. They were so united in how they spoke and wrote that it seemed as though only one person was writing, despite their unconventional methods. She had started three stories while Victor was gone and Jack was working in the north, but they had all petered out before she'd had very much of the story.

Violet applied her makeup slowly, blending the rouge into her cheeks and muting the too-bright rouge with a light layer of powder. She wasn't intending to leave the house that evening, but sometimes just the process of playing with makeup was soothing. She finished her face off with a deep red lip and drawn on brows. Sniffing at the faded headache and testing the idea of food against the feel of her stomach, she took the first dress from her closet. It was a drop waist with loose sleeves to her elbow and the color of rust. Vi couldn't quite decide if it set off her complexion or made her look yellow. She suspected the question itself was reason enough not to wear the dress again, but she slipped it over her head regardless.

After dressing, Violet strolled down to the parlor for tea and found that Kate had not awoken, but Lila and Denny had arrived. They were leaning back in the parlor entirely at home.

CHAPTER THREE

"*D*on't speak to me," Violet told Denny with a scowl. "I never should have let you talk me into so many mint juleps."

He grinned lazily. "Did you not have a remedy this morning?"

"You know," she pronounced with a narrowed gaze, "as we discussed it last night, that Mr. Giles—the genius of remedies—has been gallivanting about in his home village or some such while Victor was honeymooning."

Denny giggled, glancing at Lila as though he'd pulled a clever stunt.

Violet's scowl deepened. "Did you *entrap* me?"

"You made your own choices, dear Vi," Denny said, while the twinkle in his eye told another story. Violet recalled the number of drinks he'd pressed into her hands the previous evening. Denny had seemed helpful at the time. She should have known instantly he was up to something.

He crossed to the tea tray and loaded a plate with biscuits and sandwiches and then propped his feet up as he leaned back on the sofa. He popped the entirety of a smoked salmon sandwich in his mouth before settling his plate on his lap.

"Oh, laddie," Lila said with a sigh as she watched her husband hardly chew the sandwich. "Feel free to get your vengeance, darling Vi. Maybe after we're sure he's not choking. I'm not ready to be a widow. Turn your attention this way, darling. We do come with the most delightful information."

Violet lifted a single brow and sipped her tea, channeling her stepmother.

"Turn off that Lady Eleanor nonsense, darling one," Lila said, kicking Denny when he started to speak. "You remember Denny's brother?"

"The soot-covered one?"

"He's quite the knowledgeable young man. He's coming here, darling."

"Here?" Violet rubbed her brow.

"Here. I do hope you don't mind. I told him you'd be ever so helpful."

"Me?" Violet demanded. "Why? Does he need investment advice?"

"Denny told Wendell you were helpful. Your *father* told Greyly —that's Wendell's patron—you were ever so clever."

"My father doesn't care that Aunt Agatha trained me in investing," she said, while wondering who Wendell and Greyly were and what they had to do with her. She felt as though she were missing part of the conversation that might be important.

Lila laughed as Denny said around his sandwich, "Darling Vi —" He swallowed and then finished. "No one cares about that. Your father told Greyly all about you meddling in all those investigations and discovering killers. Sometimes even ahead of Jack. The earl loves that part."

"What Greyly loves, however," Lila said, leaning back and biting her lip to hide her smile, "is Jack."

"He's not alone there," Violet replied. "Has he *met* Jack?"

"He's heard of him. After your father told him all about you with a side of Jack. It seems Mr. Greyly focused on Jack. He went and talked to Barnes this morning."

"Because of the fires at his properties?"

"Mmmm," Lila nodded. "Denny told his brother that you were brilliant at ferreting out secrets and crimes. Whereupon, Mr. Greyly lifted his prodigious brows and harrumphed as Denny said you were just the one—"

Violet closed her eyes and took a long sip of her tea, considering sending someone for more aspirin. "What now?"

"You darling, you're just the one!"

Violet rubbed her temples. "My head still hurts, Lila."

She blinked rapidly, trying to do something about her dry eyes and slowly turned her gaze to Denny. Violet flinched from the sight of Denny shoving another sandwich into his mouth. He shrugged at her flabbergasted expression and then ate another sandwich, moaning at the perfect mix of herbs, cucumber, and butter.

"It goes like this," Lila said very slowly. "Denny's brother, Wendell—"

"Wendell?" Violet repeated.

"Isn't it a delightful name?" Turning to Denny she said, "Darling, we should start making a list of terrible names to give our children."

"We should," he said around his sandwich. "This is why we're in love, sweet perfect wife."

Lila scowled at her husband and then returned to talking slowly to Violet.

"So, Wendell is an archeologist who started working for a

fellow this last year. He's been somewhere...you know...far away and dirty."

"This is the sooty brother?"

"Yes," Lila answered. "He's just returned to England with a few of the other grubby fellows. They're all coming in from wherever this patron has been supporting digs."

"That's what they're called," Denny added. "Digs."

Violet rolled her eyes. "Even I knew that, love."

"So, Greyly wants to have a show of what he's discovered."

Violet shrugged, somewhat intrigued by the idea while also being entirely uncaring. If her head wasn't hurting quite so much, she might have been interested whether they were digging in Greece, in Turkey, or in Egypt. She might have even been persuaded to visit such a show.

"However," Lila said in that slow drawl, "there was that fire yesterday. There's been a few more fires, actually. The diggers are coming in to London and with their arrivals—fires!"

"Fires?" Violet asked, rubbing her eyes again. Her headache was fading as intrigue grew.

"Fires! Wendell showed up at our door once again today along with the patron of the digging—Greyly. It seems Greyly shared a pipe with your father last night."

"Did he?" Violet sipped her tea as she considered. She'd poured herself Earl Grey tea as a comfort. Her stomach hadn't settled yet and the idea of a liver pâté sandwich made her feel quite ill. Tea was just the thing. Perhaps a dry piece of toast. "This soot-covered, working brother is a story made up to tease me while I am unwell."

"I assure you," Lila said seriously, "we are *quite* convinced Wendell is a changeling. My darling Vi, he's earnest, knowledgeable, *and* hardworking. Babes were switched at birth."

20

"Earnest?" Vi demanded. "That doesn't sound right. He's *Denny's* brother."

"I know!" Lila's eyes sparkled with mischief. "I swear it's true."

"Knowledgeable?"

Denny cleared his throat. "Young Wendell has an article in some journal or other. I'd read it, but I'm not sure where you'd even find such a thing."

"Well," Violet told him, "perhaps if young Wendell were writing about chocolate you'd bother to discover this article."

"Indeed." Denny crossed his legs. "I thought Victor was back. I could do with a cocktail, and I prefer when they are delivered by him as though on wings. As for Wendell, far better to bend that brainwork towards something of value—like chocolate."

"All I've heard so far is that you supposedly have a brother named W*endell*—we shall now call him Wendy, I think."

"Yes. Do." Denny rose and moaned at the effort. "G&Ts, Vi? Lila, love?"

She shook her head, and Denny lifted a brow at Violet, who also declined. Vi had a firm rule of not drinking cocktails when she still felt quite sick from the last round. She really should consider avoiding becoming zozzled again.

"There have been too many fires." Lila continued the story to the sound of ice clinking and rustling near the bar. "There was another fire in a warehouse near Dover. This morning's fire was in the offices of the archeological company, and they've gotten word that there was a fire at Greyly's home in the country as well. Do you believe it?" Lila bounced on her chair, a smile on her lips. She was entirely unconcerned with whatever had been lost and far more intrigued by what had led to the slew of arson.

"My father told Greyly about me?" Violet scoffed, focusing on that part of the conversation.

"At the club, over cigars no doubt and port. Don't you think port?"

Violet did think port, but she simply lifted a brow and waved them on.

"Wendy and Greyly showed up at the door this morning when I was just settling into my nosh and begged an introduction. Somehow Greyly discovered we could introduce them to you, and the next thing you know, they came over to us posthaste and pleaded for help."

"You were coming anyway"—Violet scowled at Denny—"to see the effects of your machinations last night."

"I was," he agreed happily. "Does your head hurt much?"

Violet grabbed an embroidered pillow and threw it at Denny.

"So, after spending my breakfast with this Greyly, I knew my day wouldn't be complete if I didn't get to introduce you." The glee in Denny's voice had Violet glancing between the two of them. No doubt Lila had been convinced to not say anything about whatever was happening just so Denny could enjoy it more.

"You have to tell her the other bit," Lila told Denny.

He squirmed a bit and then admitted, "I telegraphed Jack."

"He's working," Violet said, setting down her tea to stare at Denny. "A mother of four children was murdered. Her youngest child is a baby. Only a few months old."

Denny's gaze widened. "Vi— Jack is quite a bit larger than me."

Vi's gaze narrowed further.

He shuffled and then cleared his throat. "Look, Vi. You know if it were me, I'd let you get into whatever trouble you wanted. I'd endorse the trouble. *You* know this. But...also...Jack...so, so big."

"Dear *Wendy* and his patron want to invite you to a Bonfire Night party. The old guy..." Lila glanced at Denny. Denny examined another sandwich before eating only half of it with a single bite.

"He thinks that the suspects will be at the party." The way Lila said it had Violet's head tilting as she examined her friend. Lila glanced at Denny and then winced dramatically.

"Is *Wendy* a suspect?"

"What? No!" Denny said as Lila nodded and winked both eyes alternatively.

"Ohhhhh," Violet cooed. The last of her blues faded and her headache transitioned to the back of her head. Violet downed all of her tea. "Do tell me more about this criminal brother."

"No!" Denny squeaked. "Never Wendell. You'll break my mother's heart, and *I'll* never hear the end of it. Never. Even if it *is* Wendy, it's not Wendy. Whatever you need, Vi. Pin it on someone else."

Violet stared at Denny. He scowled back at her, and they engaged in a stare-down that he immediately lost.

"Look," he said placatingly. "Look. Let me explain. Wendy... ah...Wendell, damn it! He's a good kid. The *one* kid. My parents aren't proud *of me*. If they lose Wendy—ah, Wendell—damn it, Violet. You're a devil. How did you do that so fast?"

"So this Greyly wants me to come to this Bonfire Night event and just *know* who is setting these fires?"

Denny grinned at Violet. "When I told him I'd send for Jack, Greyly seemed relieved. He doesn't have the same faith in you that I do. You're a female."

Violet leaned slowly forward, sniffing. Denny laughed and then shoved his empty plate aside. "I didn't say *I* had the same prejudices. Wendell is terrified of Lila, so he doesn't have those assumptions either."

"On the one hand," Violet told Lila, "my father praised me well enough that someone wanted our services."

Lila nodded, taking Denny's cocktail from him and sipping it. "On the other hand, these fellows wanted Jack. Denny included."

Violet took the cocktail from Lila, downing it, then winced. "Oh, I shouldn't have finished the cocktail. I broke all rules about drinking when I don't feel well. I am both personally offended at their lack of faith in the human race and personally happy to hear that Jack is returning."

"He might not come," Lila mused.

Denny groaned. "Of course he'll come. The only reason he took the job far away is that the earl can be terrifying."

"What now?" Lila and Violet demanded.

"Please," Denny said. "Jack got told to keep his hands to himself until after the wedding day. Much easier to do when the twin is lurking. Victor—well—he's not going to make things easy for Jack, now, is he? Especially since there is no way Victor didn't get his own chat with Daddy Lancaster."

"What in the world?" Violet asked Lila.

"Darling," Lila laughed, "allow me to translate. Victor has been protecting your virtue. Both of your boys were threatened, Victor to keep you pure and Jack to—" Lila shrugged and tilted her head. "Well, I suppose, to also keep you pure. Especially, of course, because if Isolde hasn't dipped her toe into the marital bed early, I'll eat my hat."

"Lila!" Violet gasped.

"You can tell by how he touches her."

"What?" Violet breathed. "Really."

"Strung tight, is our Jack," Denny agreed. "Poor fellow."

"This conversation is entirely untoward," Violet declared, knowing she was blushing a brilliant red. "Isolde?"

Lila nodded and Violet touched her fingers to her collar bone where it had once broken.

"Regardless," Denny said idly. "Jack is attempting to respect your father, so when Victor left, Jack left too. Your twin is many things—including the lesser twin—but he's an excellent chastity belt when it comes to you."

Violet stared between her two friends with their twitching lips, certain faces, and laughing gazes and then set her teacup down with a click.

"That is enough of this conversation," Violet said, knowing that if anything, her blush had deepened to a furious beet red. "You all are bad influences. You both—terrible—I—I hate you."

CHAPTER FOUR

"*My* lady?" Violet looked over to the doorway where Hargreaves stood. She was still blushing from Denny's comments, and Hargreaves paused before his face smoothed into a perfect calm.

"Yes, Hargreaves?" Violet asked, as though she weren't seventeen shades of red.

"There is a Mr. Harvey Greyly here for you."

Denny giggled.

"And a Wendell Lancaster."

Denny snorted and then choked on his laughter. "I am so excited." He rubbed his hands together happily. "Lila, darling, this is going to be delightful."

Lila replied smoothly, "I suspect it will be delightful, indeed."

"Well, now," Violet said to Hargreaves. "I suppose we should deal with whatever this will be. Mr. Hargreaves, would you please get Victor. Once he's joined us, show our guests into the parlor with fresh tea, and by Jove, coffee too!" Violet turned to the others. "*Is* this going to be fun? What's wrong with this fellow?"

"I suspect you won't love it as much as I do." Denny laughed. "We need Victor for this. It'll be so much better with him."

"He's hovering over Kate." Violet crossed to Denny and took his crumb-covered plate. "Brush yourself off. You look like a child who was allowed to have tea with adults."

Lila's low laugh had them both turning. Violet's gaze narrowed, but Lila wouldn't explain. Violet glanced back to Denny, who was staring at his wife. She winked at him.

Victor came in before there was anything more than mad giggles from Denny. Denny crossed to Victor, and they hugged as though they'd been separated for decades rather than a fortnight.

"This is going to be fun!" Denny told Victor as they hugged. "Violet is going to *love* Greyly."

"Ah," Lila cooed, "brotherly love. So precious. Heartwarming."

"What all this, then?" Victor asked as they finished awkwardly clapping each other on the backs and stepped away. "Something about a brother?"

"Denny has a hardworking and *earnest* brother," Violet announced.

"Who? Wendell?" Victor demanded. "The one who was always in the dirt?"

"He's an archeologist now," Denny told Victor, who nodded as though he could imagine nothing else.

"Why would he be here? Hargreaves said your brother was here with some old guy."

"That's Greyly."

Hargreaves brought in a fresh tea trolley with both tea and coffee, and Violet sighed in relief. She could use quite an excessive amount of coffee.

Victor settled himself near Violet, who explained: "This hardworking and earnest brother, whom we shall forever call Wendy but who is named Wendell, works for a fellow named Harvey Greyly, who has Denny in giggles."

"The archeologist," Victor announced.

Violet looked to Lila, who was staring in shock, and Denny, who seemed entirely unsurprised.

"The archeologist," Violet agreed, "has experienced a series of odd fires and wants Jack to resolve them. Father told this archeology fellow *I* was quite talented, but Greyly ensured that Jack would be on his way."

"Jack? Isn't he in the north of England? Or was it the Cotswolds? A murder case, yes? I understood he was expected to be gone quite a bit longer."

"As well as preserving my virtue," Violet agreed, as she crossed her legs and lifted a brow at her brother, who blushed and glanced away. So he knew exactly why Jack had left. Her gaze narrowed on him, but he avoided her eyes perfectly. Which was fine. She'd find him when he wasn't suspecting it and pin him down.

Victor choked on his laugh as the door opened and the two men entered. Victor and Denny rose while Lila moved to the seat directly next to Violet. Introductions were made and then Mr. Greyly looked to Wendell.

Violet whispered, "By the heavens! He looks just like Denny used to, except for smart."

Wendell was a couple of inches taller than Denny and stronger. Wendell looked as though he'd been digging in the dirt, and his shoulders were nearly as broad as Jack's. With a deep tan, the man looked like a healthy version of Denny.

"He's lovely isn't he?" Lila whispered back with a little growl in her voice. Her gaze was fixated on her brother-in-law.

"Turn your eyes away," Violet hissed. "You're in love with his *brother*. You're considering becoming a mother. Eyes away!"

"He's just a pretty face. I don't *want* him. It's like looking back in time, but maybe a little better. He wouldn't make me laugh though."

"Lady Violet," Mr. Greyly announced, clearing his throat to draw her attention, "was our plight explained to you? Can we count on your Mr. Wakefield to arrive and assist?"

Victor choked and Denny giggled.

"Mmm," Violet said, pouring a cup of tea for Wendell Lancaster. She should have poured for Greyly first, but he was annoying Violet. "I haven't spoken to Jack."

"But your friends have?"

Violet shrugged. Denny had sent Jack a telegram. Violet had little doubt that Jack would come. Denny was a dramatic fellow in between naps, and he would have worded the telegram in the right way to get Jack to return to London.

Violet sighed as she studied Mr. Greyly. "What is it about your case, I wonder, that is more important than the murder case that Jack is working?"

Mr. Greyly blinked rapidly. "I'm afraid you don't understand the importance of our work." He gestured at the men as if asking them to explain things to the simple female.

Violet slowly turned to Lila and saw that Denny had bitten his bottom lip to hold back his reaction.

"I feel certain, however," Violet told him archly, "that I under-stand the importance of human life."

"They're already gone, aren't they? This is a crime in progress."

Violet lifted a brow, but Mr. Greyly was entirely unaffected. "Well," she said, "your manipulations have, I'm sure, been successful. Mr. Wakefield will no doubt arrive sooner rather than later."

"I—find myself surprised by you, my dear," Mr. Greyly said.

"Do you?"

Mr. Greyly's reply was another harrumph, after which he turned to Victor and made a comment on the weather.

Wendy was looking distinctly uncomfortable. A blush was spreading across his face, and Violet felt a flash of sympathy. The poor man's blush only intensified as he realized Denny was in his armchair, fighting hysterical laughter.

Given that they were sent off to school at rather young ages, and Wendell was quite a bit younger than Denny—well...how much did they really know each other? Poor Wendy had no idea what he was dealing with.

Violet's head cocked, watching the brothers interact more than listening to Mr. Greyly talk. He had a loud, brash voice. His hair was mostly gone but what was left was combed over his head.

"Who do you think is setting the fires?" Violet finally asked Mr. Greyly, who smiled at her in a condescending way. Violet barely bit back her scoff and eye roll. She knew that was *why* he wanted Jack's investigative skills, but surely Mr. Greyly had suspicions.

"Well now, my dear," Mr. Greyly said. "Don't worry over it. Your Mr. Wakefield will be here soon, I assume."

Violet's face smoothed into a polite smile. "Lovely weather we're having." Greyly scowled her direction and then frowned, glancing at the window where the rain was pattering against the glass.

"Can you believe this weather?" Victor added with a mischievous gleam. "Makes the traffic almost impossible."

As Mr. Greyly looked at Victor in alarm, Violet poured him a cup of tea and asked if he wanted milk or sugar. He shook his head, distracted, and while he was looking away, Violet loaded his tea with rather a lot of sugar and handed it over. He accepted the tea and glanced again at the window.

"So happy to hear Mr. Wakefield is coming," Mr. Greyly said

with a trace of concern. "I've been reading about Mr. Wakefield and Mr. Barnes. Had my secretary gather up what could be found about them. There was quite an interesting article in the Piccadilly Press. About you too, but I understand E. Allen is a woman. Must understand hyperbole with you ladies. Take it with a grain of salt, am I right?" His chuckle burst out, and he looked at Victor and Denny for a laugh, but all he got was a nervous giggle from Denny, who immediately glanced at Vi, noted her dangerous expression and the way she handed him his tea, tipping the tea cup threateningly over his trousers. He accepted the cup and smiled quietly instead into the milky and sweet coffee.

Violet's eye twitched as Lila choked back a laugh.

Victor shifted. "Well, where do your suspicions lie with who might be setting the fires?"

Mr. Greyly harrumphed. "It has to be someone or a set of someones who have been at all of our locations."

Violet bit down on the inside of her mouth to just prevent herself retorting, 'Obviously.' Her brother smiled engagingly at Greyly's answer to Victor's question—the same Violet had asked.

"Is there a list of individuals who meet that criteria?" Victor asked, after meeting Violet's gaze and grinning at her.

Violet poured herself a cup of coffee and leaned back, sipping. Her gaze narrowed on Mr. Greyly as he glanced her way. "Smile, my dear, you're far too pretty for such a frown." He took a long sip of tea and paused as the sugary taste hit his mouth.

Violet slowly blinked, but Denny burst into laughter.

"Have I said something funny, then?" Mr. Greyly frowned at Denny. "He's really quite a bit different from you, isn't he, Lancaster?"

"I understand that Wendell is earnest and hardworking. Quite brilliant, even." Violet tilted her head as she watched Greyly glance at Wendell and then lift one of those giant brows.

"That might be going a bit far, but he is a handy man to have about." Mr. Greyly set his tea aside after shooting Violet another fierce frown.

"Even if he's only useful, he's quite the opposite from Denny."

It took Mr. Greyly a moment to realize she'd insulted Denny, and Greyly's frown deepened.

Denny winked at Violet as he said, "I'm confused, Mr. Greyly, did you want Vi's help? I assume that's why you wanted me and my wife to introduce you. I'm sure you heard when we explained that she is rather brilliant at ferreting out criminals herself."

"But of course those cases were solved by Mr. Wakefield. I mean, Miss Violet, you couldn't have had much to do with it? You're a woman!"

"I am a woman," Vi said smoothly. "Brilliant of you to notice, and it's Lady," she said, smoothly sipping her tea.

"I'm sorry?" Greyly replied.

"Lady. Miss Violet is incorrect."

"Ah, of course. Apologies."

Violet set her coffee down, losing patience with Greyly as he again glanced to Denny and Victor as if to say, 'What else could you expect from a woman?'

"Mr. Wakefield isn't here. Why don't I have him call you once he returns to the city?"

"I hope we can expect you at our Bonfire Night party," Greyly said, instead of taking the hint. Violet glanced at Lila and towards the door as Greyly continued. "There will be quite a display of the things we've discovered on our digs, won't there be, Lancaster? Quite an exciting evening even for you, Miss...ah... Lady Violet."

Her gaze flicked to her brother and her brow lifted in a silent order, which he immediately understood.

"You know," Victor said, "I must apologize and ask you to

excuse the ladies. Their assistance is required at a local charity event."

"Of course, of course," Mr. Greyly said, harrumphing again. His gaze dropped down Violet's body and then slid to Lila where his focus lingered on her chest. Violet rose and pulled Lila up after.

"So nice meeting you," she lied. "So nice of you to invite us to your party where you'll be able to tell us all about you." She smiled at Mr. Greyly, ignoring Wendy's gasp and Denny's giggle. "Let's go, love. Maybe we can find a new dress to be pretty for all the men at Mr. Greybull's party."

"It's Greyly," he said.

"Oh, of course. So nice meeting you, Wendy, Mr. Greybull."

Lila let Violet pull her from the room and then burst into laughter in the hallway. "How many sugars did you put in his tea?"

"I don't know," Violet told her. "Women can't count. You know that. Probably two. Maybe six."

Lila laughed harder, and together they ran up the stairs towards Kate and Victor's room, pushing through the door. Violet heard the sound of sicking up and glanced back at Lila. "Let's going shopping without her then?"

"Oh, I think so." Lila stepped back into the hallway on a particularly vicious gagging noise.

"I'll send Beatrice in."

"It's why you pay her so well."

"Still thinking about procreating?" Violet demanded, when they'd silently pulled the door shut behind themselves.

"Mmm," Lila mused, as Kate gagged ferociously in the bath. "Perhaps in another year or two."

"We might as well let Victor and Kate pave the way for us. Make the mistakes first, you know. Go through all the wrong nannies. We'll steal theirs by paying them double once they've found a good one."

They ran across the hall to Violet's room, and Lila spun when they reached the door. "Are you still blue?"

Violet shook her head.

"Because Jack is coming home?"

"Because we're going to that party, and we're going to spend the entire time ensuring that Mr. Greyly never—"

"I think you mean Mr. Greybull."

"—never," Violet continued as though Lila had not spoken, "underestimates a woman again. We can't work with Jack this time. It's you and me and Kate, should she stop sicking up."

Lila grinned. "I would suggest it might interfere with my nap, but I'll be going to a party on Bonfire Night either way. I would, however, prefer to be going to the scavenger hunt with actual friends."

"Ooh," Violet said, as she opened the door to her room and found Beatrice straightening her closet. "Darling Beatrice. Would you look after Kate? I fear that Victor moaning along with her isn't going to help her feel better."

Beatrice agreed and left the room.

Violet faced Lila. "I know I came back with all the clothes the stores had yesterday, but today I feel certain that I will need a more dazzling dress for this Bonfire Night party."

"Perhaps something with beading."

"Yes, flashy for certain. You're going to be dazzling too. Something with a low cut v-neck for you, dear Lila. Greybull does enjoy your chest."

Lila gasped, and then laughed when Denny stuck his head in the door. "Greyly left. Wendy—Wendell—is still here. Come meet my brother and ask him the questions Greyly wouldn't answer. Victor and I would, of course—but let's be real here. I don't have any idea of what to ask, and Victor is the lesser twin."

Violet grinned at him, and he grinned back.

"You're the best, Vi."

She shrugged.

"He was terrible."

She nodded.

"That was just wonderful, just wonderful. I'm not sure I've ever enjoyed a tea with you so much. When he answered Victor's question that you had just asked. By Jove! I think you had steam coming from your ears, dear one. It was fabulous."

"Violet put six sugars in Greybull's tea." Lila laughed.

"How many did he ask for? No one actually asks for that many."

"None."

"Your comment on the weather, and the look on his face after Victor bemoaned the downpour. I do love you, Vi," Denny pronounced.

CHAPTER FIVE

"So you're the hardworking brother?" Violet asked, as she re-entered the parlor. "Make me an Old-Fashioned, Victor. Make it strong, please."

"Weren't you at a charity event?" Wendy asked. "I apologize, I thought you left. Then Denny told me to sit tight, and—I don't want to keep you from the orphans or the wounded soldiers. I'm sure you must be up to something important."

"Shopping," Violet agreed with a nod. "Though Victor and I do support an orphanage in your hometown."

"I—" Wendy looked to Denny and back to Violet. The poor man's mouth was hanging a little open.

"He is earnest," Violet told Lila as they hooked arms. "I like him."

"I—" Wendy glanced around the room as if surprised. "Is this really how you *live?*"

"It is," Victor said as he handed everyone an Old-Fashioned. "We are frivolous and merry and lazy."

"Just so lazy."

"We are indeed," Violet told the man. "No one is quite as lazy as dear Denny. I think, Wendy, that you received all of the capacity your family had to provide for hard work."

"It's Wendell."

"Your Greyly is horrible," Violet told the man.

"Yes. I'm—ah—aware that Mr. Greyly can be—ah, difficult. I mean. I—"

"Denny, you would say anything," Victor told Denny. "What's wrong with your brother?"

"I think he has manners," Lila said. "We're all surprised."

Violet sighed. "You're educated. Why are you putting up with Greyly?"

"Archeology is expensive. It's the pursuit of something ancient and wonderful for the knowledge. The expansion of where we came from, of what we're capable of. It only happens when people like Greyly with money to spare get involved. You...you... they're..."

"They're necessary," Violet finished for Wendy, meeting his earnest gaze. "By Jove! You are hardworking. Who do you think is setting these fires?"

"Greyly is terrible. So anyone might. He...he makes you put all journal articles past him so he can adjust for his own theories. He...he takes credit for the best finds. He ruins you if you leave his projects. Not that anyone else would hire you if you've worked for Greyly."

"You seem upset," Violet said.

Wendy paled. "Well. I am. It's just—we all are."

Violet sipped her drink. "All of you?"

He nodded.

"And who has been here who could have done this?"

"Every archeologist coming in for the party and probably their assistants. Anyone who wants a job for a more reputable man. Greyly sucks you into this madness and then owns your life and your career."

"So you went to school, studied, got a job and thought, 'By Jove! I've made it!' Only to have all of your dreams crash apart once you realized what you got pulled into?"

He nodded, glancing to the side. "It's amazing when you're digging and finding things. It's awful when Greyly takes your discoveries and ruins everything."

Violet's head tilted as she examined Wendell Lancaster. He was Kate's cousin, Denny's little brother, and something of an enigma. His eyes fixed on hers, but unlike Denny's, they were bright. Wendy had set his cocktail immediately aside. He was hiding his emotions, desperately trying to hold them back. They were Denny's eyes though. "How much do you hate him?" Violet asked him.

Denny laughed and lifted his cocktail to his brother and then wound his fingers through Lila's. "What do you think? Is he ready for Violet?"

"I still see him as the grubby little boy who was digging in the garden. I don't know."

"I don't understand why you're making a big deal about her," Wendy said. "I—don't believe—I—look—I have met many brilliant women."

Violet lifted a brow.

"Here's the thing about Vi," Denny told Wendy expansively. "She's more clever than you'd think."

"No—no offense, Lady Vi—but Mr. Greyly is counting on, ah, well, your fiancé."

"Use your imagination, my lad!" Denny called fervently before swallowing the rest of his cocktail. "You think that because Vi is all pretty and feminine and has those big eyes and fluttery lashes that she's not two steps ahead of you?"

Wendell scowled at Denny. "This is all very untoward, Denny."

"Maybe it's because she smells good," Lila suggested. "He can't handle how good she smells, I think."

Victor scoffed.

"She doesn't smell as good as you, Lila love. It's the eyes. She stares off into the distance and we lads think, what if she's dreaming of me?"

"Lila Junior," Lila said immediately. "Or Jack Junior. We'll call him J.J. except for Violet, who will always call him something entirely frivolous. Like Teddy Bear."

"Is this how you really talk?" Wendell asked. "And how you spend your days now that you have the money from our aunt? You're all idiots."

"Not Vi," Denny and Lila said together and then laughed when Wendell stared at them as though he couldn't believe they were serious.

Denny yawned aggressively then whined, "When is Jack coming? I feel like I can't leave Violet to her shenanigans until Jack appears."

"She needs a keeper?" Wendy demanded.

"No," Violet and Lila said, as Victor and Denny said, "Yes."

Violet's gaze narrowed on the lads, who grinned at her, but neither took back their assertion.

"Vi, love," Victor said, patting her hand. "There was that time at Christmas. You couldn't move freely for weeks."

Violet turned to Lila, who was shaking her head at both Victor and Denny, wincing dramatically for them.

"Come on, Vi," Denny said. "You've cut it close a few times, is all. You know? Added a little spice to your life, perhaps. It's just..."

"Jack," Lila said for her husband.

"He's just quite large," Denny added. "Protective."

"He could squash Denny like a bug and not even breathe heavily afterwards."

"I could do that," Violet told Lila.

She considered for a moment and then grinned at Violet, shrugging and nodding. "Yes, darling. I think you could. It's your killer instinct. Denny's all spaniel. You're like a lioness. One of those big African cats."

"I can't even tell what you're talking about anymore," Wendell said. "I have serious business." He stood and nodded at the women before scowling at his brother and stating, "Thank you for your time."

Denny laughed as his brother stalked out of the parlor and then turned an expectant gaze on Violet as she took the final sip of her cocktail.

"Well," Violet said, "shall we go dress shopping then, Lila?"

"Indeed," she nodded. "Victor. Laddie."

They had a black cab called while they gathered their coats and cloches, and then the two of them slipped into the backseat of the car, sending the driver towards the British Museum.

"How long do you think it'll take them to realize we didn't go shopping?" Lila asked.

"Denny? He probably won't realize at all."

"And Victor?" Lila demanded.

"He already knows." Violet crossed her leg in the car and shivered into her coat. It was quite damp, and the rain was coming down in sheets.

The black cab stopped in front of the British Museum, and

they hurried inside. Violet approached the ticket box. "Are there any archeologists here?"

The man adjusted his jacket and looked down his nose at her.

Violet took his condescending expression as a yes and said, "Would you tell them that Lady Violet Carlyle is here? I'd be willing to entertain the idea of a contribution to their work should they be willing to entertain my questions."

"Lady Violet Carlyle?" He didn't believe her.

"Lady Violet Carlyle," Violet replied. "Why don't you tell them and let them be the judges?"

He narrowed his gaze on her, but Violet tilted her head, lifted a brow, and channeled her stepmother. She felt as though she'd put an invisible tiara on, but it worked. The man blushed and nodded once and said something to another fellow to watch the ticket box.

Violet and Lila crossed to a bench and seated themselves until a small man in brown tweed appeared with the ticket man. The man in brown tweed glanced Lila and Violet over. "Lady Violet?"

"That would be me," Violet replied. She rose and held out her hand, letting the little fellow in tweed squeeze her fingers. "May I introduce my good friend, Mrs. Lila Lancaster?"

He nodded and then said, "I am Henry Parker. Ah, this is very awkward. I understood that you offered a bit of support for our work?"

"Perhaps," Violet said with a smile. "I would be willing, but I do have some questions."

The man accepted.

"Will you tell me what you do here?"

Mr. Parker went through the process of his work as he led her through the museum, and Violet had to force herself to turn away from scenes of astounding beauty to focus on the man. His work focused on the discoveries that were pulled from Egypt. After they had a rapport running, Violet asked him, "What do you know of Harvey Greyly?"

Parker scoffed. "That hack? He's just rich with his own wild theories. Legitimate archeologists won't work with him."

"What about young archeologists who don't know better?"

Parker shrugged. "No one else hires Greyly's hacks. They destroy their reputation. They destroy their legitimacy. There are more who want to dig than can afford it."

"What if they're still very young?" Lila demanded. "Earnest. Hardworking?"

"Again, my dear," Mr. Parker cut in, "there are more men who want to dig than can be hired for it."

He led them into his office and offered them a seat.

Violet crossed her hands over her stomach. "Tell me about those who work for Greyly."

"I don't know much of them," Parker said.

Violet laughed merrily. "Mr. Parker, archeology is like being a member of the upper crust. The circle is small, and we all know each other better than we'd prefer. Surely you're the same?"

Parker glanced at Violet and Lila. "Greyly has good men working for him. He manipulates their findings to support his theories. His archeologists hate him. Some of them hate him but still want to work. Stephen Lands is writing a book to counteract Greyly for when Lands retires. It won't reverse the damage of all he's done, but I think Lands mostly cares about the message he intends to send to Greyly."

Violet lifted a brow. "What about the other fellows who work for Greyly?"

"Why do you care?"

"He's had a series of fires," Violet said.

"And why does that concern you, *Lady* Violet?"

Violet smiled merrily. "You make a good point, sir. It doesn't concern me. It does, however, concern a friend. It's important to me to understand why this series of fires is happening."

There were small crates sitting on the shelf behind Parker's desk, and she could see that he'd been working on something small and engraved. Was it a coin? Some piece of jewelry? What was it that he was seeing in the object? Some piece of history that explained its use or significance?

Violet took a deep breath in. "To tell you the truth, Mr. Parker, I don't really care who is setting these fires. I'm not emotionally attached to any of the destroyed objects, and I'm not obsessed with the past. The losses, whatever they are—"

"They're priceless!"

"Are they? While I do find what you are doing here interesting, I am far more intrigued by *why* you care more about what you discover than exactly what you uncover. I suppose I'm more intrigued by the living than those who have gone before."

"Then why did you offer to finance my work? Why are you here to find out about this? Are you just pulling my leg?"

"What if I were to tell you that I would donate to your next dig as long as you took on one of Greyly's men?"

"I would tell you that my work is more important than your money."

"What if I were to ask you simply to give him a chance?"

"Has he published?"

"I believe so." Violet took a deep breath in and then admitted, "I'm very rich, Mr. Parker. May I share with you that I can donate to your cause, or I can finance a dig. A dig that comes along with Wendell Lancaster. Perhaps you'd like to go to Greyly's Bonfire Night party and see what you think of the lad?"

"I wasn't invited."

"Would you like to be my date?"

Lila choked, biting down on her lip.

"I—" Mr. Parker nodded once.

Handing Parker a card, Violet winked at him and said, "I'll see you then, my friend. If you want to have a dig financed, you should be prepared to astound me with what I'm seeing and bond with Wendell Lancaster."

"And if I don't?"

"But you do."

CHAPTER SIX

*R*ouge licked Violet awake the next morning. Vi shoved her spaniel back and then shoved back her eye mask. She blinked blearily towards the window and saw that Beatrice had been in the room. Violet must have been pretty tired for the maid to succeed in sneaking in, lighting the fire, cracking the curtains, and escaping. The rain was pounding against the window panes, and Violet smiled at it.

She felt a rush of pure joy. She hadn't had one bad dream the previous night. Was that why she felt amazing this morning? Or was it because she'd returned to find a telegram from Jack that he was on his way.

Violet smiled over the very simple message.

WILL RETURN ON 4th. JACK

The back of her mind was in a full duel about whether she should be so happy he was returning if she was an independent woman. Maybe it was more that the despondency she'd been experiencing was gone as well. What if her blues had gone because of Jack? If so, was she terribly dependent upon him? She had to remind herself, however, that her spirits had lifted when her interest had been piqued by the fires.

"Girl," Violet told Rouge, "you've got to do something about these blues."

She pulled out her journal and started flipping back through the pages to see when they'd struck this last time. It took a few minutes to realize that they'd started two days after everyone had left. She frowned, feeling rather weak to realize that being alone had pushed her into such melancholy.

What was she going to do about it? That *ennui* was driving her mad. She flipped through her journal, looking for the days she'd felt better, searching for what had been different. It took her a long while to realize she felt better when she had her jiu-jitsu lessons and when she took Rouge out for walks.

"Walks are the answer?"

Rouge's tail flapped frantically against the bed, and Violet realized she'd crossed rather a terrible line with the poor dog.

"Walk?"

Rouge yipped, wagging her tail frantically with wide, pleading eyes, and Violet sighed. She was committed now, she thought, as she quickly dressed in a warm dress, wool stockings, boots, and her coat. She added a raincoat and hat and then said, "Well, come on then."

Thankfully, the small spaniel would be happy with a short walk. Violet and Rouge hurried out the door and into the rain. Victor's house was in a nice neighborhood of over-sized houses that surrounded a small park. Vi and the dog rushed across the street into the park and the dog yipped and bounced in the puddles as though the sky was raining just for Rouge to play in.

After one lap around the park, Violet headed back towards

the house and saw a black cab stopping. A very large man with quite broad shoulders got out of the black cab, and Violet stared as he stood up. He, too, was wearing a raincoat, and his gaze darted around the neighborhood with those dark, penetrating eyes.

Violet had little doubt that he noted the local bobby making his way through the beat of the neighborhood. The nanny from three doors down who was trying to get the children back inside from their own splashing in rubber boots. He didn't walk up the steps to Number 7 where Violet and Victor lived. Instead, he crossed the street to the park and stopped in front of her.

Rouge barked a frantic hello, and Violet said, "I wouldn't have thought you'd be back so quickly. It's early." She studied his face, noting the dark circles under his eyes, the tightness of his jaw, and the overall exhaustion. He looked haunted and sad. It was a state he hadn't shown after most of the other murders they'd seen. This last case must have been quite a bad one. She reached out her ungloved fingers to his and tangled them together.

"I took the night train down." He sounded husky, as though he hadn't spoken in hours.

"Are you all right?"

He shook his head. Violet stepped into his body heat, ignoring the rain and their own drenched coats.

"Is there anything I can do?"

He placed his index finger under her chin, his gaze moving over her face before he tilted it and pressed a kiss on her forehead. There was something in his gaze that made it seem as though ghosts were chasing him.

"No, darling Vi, there is nothing to be done."

Violet's mouth twisted, helpless to know how to help him. This must be how Jack felt, she thought, when he found that she was having nightmares. Or when she'd gotten herself involved in another murder case. Helpless and worried.

"Did you find the killer?"

"We knew who it was from the first. We just needed to prove it."

His tone told her who it was, but she needed him to tell her anyway. "The father? The husband?"

Jack's jaw tightened and he nodded once. "He was a monster. The children are orphans. There's no one to take them. I—Vi, they're good kids. They deserve better. That baby—she's so little. Some kindly neighbor is feeding her with her own child, but Vi. It was bad. It was so bad."

Violet's heart broke. She wasn't an orphan in the traditional sense. She had a father, a stepmother, and her great-aunt. Despite all that, she'd felt the lack of a mother keenly.

"What do you want to do?"

Jack pressed his chin on top of her head. "We can't save them all."

"Why not the ones who've already crawled into your heart? It's not like it would be the first time."

"Another Ginny?" he asked, referring to her and Victor's ward. Violet had ended up agreeing to take the girl on when her grandmother died. Violet wasn't sure she would have been capable of saying no to any child, but Ginny was a special case—she'd helped Violet save her sister from a kidnapper. "Or that other one? Mathers's little sister. I know you keep Ginny out of trouble and get the other one into it."

Violet grinned. She wasn't responsible for Anna Mathers like she was Ginny.

"We could send them to a good orphanage? Check in on them?" Jack obviously didn't like that idea, but he said it anyway.

"We could hire a nanny for them and buy a seaside cottage.

What better place to grow up than playing in the ocean? Send the children to school. We could bring them to our house. Oh! Oh, by Jove! I've got it!"

Jack pulled back. "What?"

"Kate's mother! My goodness, Jack, I bet she would raise them. If we added a governess and paying for school, getting them established somehow? We'll send Beatrice—no! Oh goodness, we should definitely have them come here. We'll have the children at...Lila and Denny's."

Jack frowned. "Why Lila and Denny? They're idiots. Though lovable idiots," he added.

"Mrs. Lancaster is a woman who takes care of things. She'll see them failing terribly at caring for the children and take over. We'll have big conversations in front of her about what we should do and maybe get her to visit some of the more horrible orphanages here."

"And what if she doesn't step up?"

"Then we'll go with plan two. If this works—" Violet glanced around to check for prying eyes and then pressed onto her toes leaving a kiss on Jack's chin as she whispered, "Victor will owe us *forever.*"

"How do you figure?"

"I think his mother-in-law is already on her way to London, Jack." Violet laughed into his chest. "They weren't even supposed to be back yet, and she's on her way."

Jack winced, and she glanced around again, checking for spies before she kissed his chin. She whispered up at him as though Victor could somehow hear. "He'd owe us *forever.*"

Some of the darkness leaked out of Jack's gaze as she grinned up at him. "We could hold it over him."

"Even Kate would appreciate it, and she loves her mother."

"We'll owe Lila and Denny," Jack said, and Violet felt the rush of shock.

They would owe Lila and Denny. Vi and Jack were becoming a —unit. She loved it. Violet grinned at him, twining her arm around his. "Shall we go have breakfast?"

"You need to warm up," he said. "Your nose is red."

"I'll take a quick bath, change my clothes, and meet you in the breakfast room."

Jack led the way up the stairs and inside the house. Hargreaves was there to take Rouge, and Violet and Jack left their wet coats with him as well. Jack tugged her into the parlor the moment Hargreaves disappeared down the hall.

"I missed you." Jack lightly drew her closer by her arm, giving her the chance to pull away, but Violet jumped into his arms and pressed her lips to his. Within moments, any remaining chill from the walk in the rain was gone.

The door to the parlor opened a moment later, and Victor called, "Jack! Here already? I didn't think you'd get here so early in the day." They shook hands, and Victor grinned. Jack had stepped back, but Violet left her hand on his chest.

Her head tilted as she examined her brother, and for once, Violet realized what he'd been doing when he appeared whenever Violet and Jack were alone. The smirk on Victor's face was just subtle enough she'd missed it every other time. Before, however, she'd been flustered. This time she'd been looking for it.

Violet glanced up at Jack, who had placed his hand over hers on his chest and answered Victor mildly. Was Jack irritated? He looked down at Violet, and his eyes glinted just enough to tell her that he was fine.

"Where's Kate?" Violet demanded.

"She's unwell," Victor said.

"Demon spawn," Violet told Jack. "Call for Lila, Victor. I need her help with a project. Also Beatrice and perhaps Hargreaves's sister."

She didn't respond to Victor's inquiring look. He had been playing games with her and Jack, and she hadn't even been aware of it. She would make this work with Mrs. Lancaster if she had to take the woman aside and bribe her.

CHAPTER SEVEN

*V*iolet wore a long, dark cream dress on Bonfire Night. The dress was covered in gold beading and embroidery, and the beads caught the light, making her shimmer. The design formed curls and lines over the simple fabric and led down into the fringe. The hem stopped above her knees, but the fringe extended to her mid calves in a zig-zag.

Violet's shoes were heeled and beaded, matching the dress. They'd been made for each other, as was the headpiece that held Violet's dark brown bob off of her face. Violet applied her makeup carefully, then added her birthday gift from Jack. The gift included a long strand of gold beads for her neck and another series of bracelets for her wrist. Vi added her gold and diamond bangles to her other wrist. Violet examined it in the mirror and then changed her mind. She switched her bracelets, so they'd be a combination of diamond bangles and gold beaded bracelets rather than all one version on each hand.

Violet wore the engagement ring from Jack on her left hand and a stack of gold bands on the middle finger of her right hand, with a gold and diamond ring on the second finger of that hand. She was glittery and sparkling, and all she needed were some earbobs to round out her jewelry. She dug through her jewelry box until she found diamond and gold chandelier earbobs.

Violet had deliberately determined to wear something shocking to the party. It was why the hem above her fringe was higher than usual, and it was why the v-cut of her dress showed the top and sides of her breasts.

Greyly, at least, had already shown he had little respect for the intelligence of a female. A nearly blinding female with the amount of gold and shimmer Violet had put on? He didn't stand a chance. Especially when you added in low party lights and fireworks. Let alone the bonfire and the heavy alcohol.

The long gold necklace somewhat masked just how much of her chest was showing with her dress, but Violet knew that the gentlemen of the party would notice. Victor would, and Vi smiled evilly at the realization. Violet applied her lipstick carefully and popped it into a gold handbag with her powder compact.

She was dressing herself alone that evening. It had taken about one-third of an explanation for Beatrice to agree to get the children and only one more moment for Beatrice to offer up her cousin, Letty, as a nanny. Mr. Giles had been telegrammed to pick up Letty on the way back to London. It was all working out, even with Lila, who wanted to try mothering on for size, and Denny, who wanted to have a reason to play in the dirt with the children and have un-mocking cocoas for every evening and every morning.

The day had been wonderful despite the rain, the worry over the children, and the fires. They hadn't talked about the murder or the fires. Instead, they'd had breakfast, lingering over the kedgeree. Jack had snoozed in a deep-seated arm chair near the fire with a Cuban pipe, and then the two of them had enjoyed a cocktail before they'd separated to dress.

The G&T had gone down particularly well when they discussed keeping Jack's rooms versus buying a house. Jack had mentioned Kate's baby without inquiring whether Violet was ready for one of her own. He more left the opening so Violet could tell him what she wanted, but she wasn't sure.

Violet shimmied and made sure her dress stayed in place, and then she pulled her fur coat on over the dress. She didn't want Jack swallowing his tongue or Victor's comments delaying them. Neither of them had been pleased to hear that Violet had made a date with the archeologist Henry Parker. She thought she'd save them from further frustration until it was too late to talk her out of it. Vi made her way down the stairs and found both Victor and Jack standing side-by-side over the little man in the tuxedo who was waiting to take her to the party.

Poor Mr. Parker looked up at her in utter relief. She was sure he was regretting his decision to help her with this case. Her gaze was merry as she glanced him over, and he was observant enough to note the riches on her fingers and throat, a silent assurance that she had the money to assist him with his work. As for Victor and Jack, she had little sympathy. The two of them had been working together to keep Violet 'pure,' and she felt they both deserved to suffer.

"Henry!" She made sure her voice was cheery and happy as walked down the stairs. Kate was standing next to Victor, somehow looking as though she glowed despite the sound of her sicking up most of the day. Vi winked at her sister-in-law and then said, "Oh, I am looking forward to this evening."

Jack and Victor both shot Violet quelling, irritated looks that she ignored. She wanted Jack to suffer—just a little—for the game he and Victor had been playing, while also plastering herself in gifts from Jack. She knew he'd get the message, and his gaze certainly fixated on her gold beads peeking out of the top of her coat.

"Lady Violet," Henry Parker squeaked. "Ah. Oh. Hello." His gaze flicked to Jack and then back to Violet. "I—"

Violet hid her grin. "See you at the party, fellas."

Before she could follow Mr. Parker out the front door, Jack snagged her wrist with just his finger. He lifted a brow, and Violet said, "Have you met Greyly yet?"

Jack shook his head.

"You'll understand, but the game is on, my friend. The game is on."

"Are we on opposite sides?" Jack asked, and she was pleased to see that whatever darkness had remained in his gaze had faded as the day had gone on.

"Do you think you can win?"

"I am the professional," he said, but he was smiling at her. The shadows had indeed fully faded, and the sheer idea of them competing over *not* a murder amused him despite Henry Parker's presence.

"You're a scary investigator, and I'm an idiot female. You'll put them on their guard, and they'll tell me things thinking I don't even understand what it means."

He laughed further, a near shout of humour that had her own eyes glinting back at him. What an utter relief to see him happy again. "You'll entrap them?"

Violet blinked innocently up at him and then shrugged. "It's not my fault they think I'm stupid because I'm wearing lipstick and a dress."

"It's their fault," Jack agreed. "I'd never fall for that."

"Which is why," she shot back, "I fell for you. It's even why Kate loves Victor."

"You know," Victor told Violet as Jack let go of her arm, "Jack is the perfect man for you. I'm about as much of a lapdog as a man can be and not even I would let my fiancé leave the house with another man."

Kate rolled her eyes and shot Violet a look, as if to ask if she could believe this nonsense. Violet clucked. Her brother was no lapdog, and Kate would do what she wanted regardless. Besides that, Jack trusted Violet, and he knew what she was up to. It helped that Henry Parker was a tiny little man with round glasses, an ill-fitting tuxedo and ink on his fingertips.

"Darling Vi," Jack said, just as Violet stepped out the front door after Mr. Parker. She turned and stuck just her head back inside the house. "Remember who you're marrying."

Violet winked at him and left with a laugh.

"I'm a little concerned," Mr. Parker said softly, "that your fiancé will take me aside and murder me."

"Oh, don't worry about that," Violet said merrily to him. "Jack would never murder anyone. He'd just scare you away. Tell me what you found out?"

"How do you know I discovered anything?"

"Small groups of people gossip, my friend. There's no way you didn't go back to your group of colleagues and discuss what was happening."

Mr. Parker blushed as he harrumphed in the back of the black cab. It took him a full minute or more to confess. "I did talk to a few people."

It was dark, so she couldn't see his face.

"Greyly has four main digs going. Mostly funded by him, but he's good at getting other wealthy folks to donate to his cause. He does things to make them happy they donated such as gifting the large donors with things from the dig or mentioning them in articles. Those four digs each have an archeologist in charge, and they're all here in London."

Violet glanced out the window. It wouldn't take too long to get to Greyly's house.

"The first is a man named Simon Jones. He's a bit of a snake. Even before Greyly hired him on, Jones had made enemies."

"Do you think he started the fires?"

"I don't know," Parker admitted. "I never understood him. It's not like he has the passion for the work. If you want an easy job, this isn't it."

"Where is he working?"

"Jones? I think he was in Mexico. Or Guatemala?"

"My friend was in Egypt. Why in totally different places?"

"Because Greyly doesn't care. He's not pursuing some great revelation, like where Troy was or whether it existed. Greyly wants a piece of history and discovery, any piece of history, any discovery, any bit of notoriety."

"What about the others?"

"There's a Richard Lovegood who works in Greece. He's older. He's not great at what he does. He does what Greyly says, writes what Greyly says. I doubt he's your fellow. Your fiancé is working this as well?"

Violet gasped as the cab driver opened the door to the cab suddenly. She hadn't felt it come to a stop. She grinned over at Parker after she stepped out and saw the house for the first time. Greyly's house was ostentatious on a level that screamed new money.

"Well, well, well, where does his money come from?"

Violet placed her hand on Parker's and followed him up the steps. Just as they stepped into the house, she looked back over her shoulder and saw Jack stepping from another black cab. He handed out Kate and then Victor followed.

Violet lifted both brows at them before stepping inside. Greyly was greeting guests as they came in, and he stopped in shock at the sight of Violet on the arm of Henry Parker.

"Where's your fiancé? Parker? What is this? Why are *you* here, Parker?"

Vi smiled at Greyly, patted him on his arm, and said, "Now, now, my good fellow. Mr. Wakefield has arrived. You'll have to see if he wants to be your girl Friday. I've decided to learn all about archeology and perhaps even steal young Lancaster from you."

She winked at him and sidled by, pulling Parker with her. After they were out of Greyly's earshot, she said, "Why does Greyly recognize and not like you?"

"You think that other archeologists just let Greyly pollute our findings and our knowledge?"

"Are you the nemesis of Greyly and his friends?" The idea gave her pause, but she covered it with laughter.

CHAPTER EIGHT

*V*iolet followed Parker through the ballroom. There were displays around the ballroom floor showing all manner of finds from around the world. There was a display with coins, some rusted and ancient looking and some polished and shining. There was another with ancient jewelry and another with knives of all kinds. Violet paused a long time as she examined them.

"What is this here?" she asked, pointing to a black blade. It looked like a piece of glass growing out of carved wood handle.

"That's obsidian," Parker said. "Those knives are very, very sharp, but brittle. They're volcanic glass."

"Do they make jewelry out of it? It's so pretty. I admit, I have black pearls, and I'm about as spoiled as they come—"

"I can see that," Parker told Violet. "Centuries from now, people will look at your jewelry and use it to make guesses about how we lived."

Violet grinned, glancing over her shoulder and finding Jack on the dance floor with a lush blonde. Given it wasn't Lila, Violet let her gaze linger for a moment.

"I want to meet the archeologists, but first, we're definitely dancing."

"I feel certain that your inspector is going to kill me." Parker glanced over his shoulder. Did he notice Jack's broad shoulders? Violet certainly did, but she wasn't sure that Parker saw them with the same appreciation.

"He might," Violet told Parker, just to watch him pale, "if he weren't an inspector—saved by the morals he espouses. Congratulations to myself," she said happily, "on the excellent man I've seduced with my wiles. Were you aware that I'm more valuable than rubies?"

Parker snorted. "That's why we're here, isn't it? You offered those rubies, and I have work that needs financed."

Violet laughed so hard, it hurt. She took hold Parker to keep herself upright and said, "Touché, my friend, touché."

Parker led her around the dance floor rather than onto it, with frequent glances towards Jack. When they reached the other side, Parker stopped. "Jones, how's the work?"

Jones was tall—taller even than Jack—and his shoulders were broader as well. Vi's brows lifted as she watched the man slowly turn to face them. He had a deep tan that shouted a life spent outdoors. "Parker. Heard you had some good finds recently."

Violet glanced past Jones's oversized shoulders. Wendell Lancaster—Denny's earnest brother—was maneuvering out of the ballroom so casually he could only be up to trouble. Violet focused on Jones, tilted her head, and asked bluntly, "Did you set the fires?"

"Me? Why would I do that?"

"You tell me."

"Why would I tell you?"

It was a good question, and Violet considered before answering. "You'd rather tell me that the Scotland Yard man brought in to find out who did this."

"I'm sure you're prettier and more agreeable than every bloke who works for Scotland Yard, but I didn't set those fires, and I don't have any reason to go after Greyly's setup here. If he hadn't hired me, it isn't like Parker and his cronies would." Jones winked at her. "I'm a bit of hack, darling." She ran her gaze over him, noting his unrepentant look as she heard Parker growl.

"You're a danger to knowledge," Parker nearly shouted.

Violet had lost interest in Jones given his attitude. If a fellow admitted the things Jones had just admitted, he didn't have a reason to go after the work Greyly was producing.

"You know who does have a reason to go after Greyly?" Jones continued. "Parker here. The man's irrationally obsessed with archeology. There's more to life than history. This is a man who doesn't see the forest for the trees."

Parker snapped something she couldn't make out. This was dissolving into an arguing match that would lead to no new information. Violet turned and saw Jack following after where Denny's little brother had gone. So, she wasn't the only one who thought the man had been acting nefariously, but Violet didn't think Jack had even met Wendell yet. What had Jack following the man, then?

Violet excused herself from the fray and followed Jack out of the ballroom. Off of the ballroom was a servants' hallway that was filled with those coming and going. One of the maids asked Violet if she needed help, but when Vi shook her head, the maid returned to her work. Violet looked for doorways, but the hall was a straight shot to a servants' staircase. Violet skipped down the steps, which came out at the end of another hall. To the right was the kitchen. To the left was yet another hallway with doors off of it.

Violet walked down the dark hallway, listening carefully for the sound of Jack's voice and found him standing at the edge of a doorway, in the shadows. She tiptoed closer and breathed, "Jack?"

"Vi? You following me?"

"Wendy."

Jack placed his hand on her hip, pulling her into the shadow of his body. She peeked around the doorway and found young, earnest, hardworking Wendell digging through the desk next to him.

Violet stepped into the office with Jack just behind her. "What's all this, then?"

Wendell gasped and spun, and Violet sighed as she saw that he had an artifact next to him.

"Is that a knife?"

He flinched. "I—ah—"

"You were supposed to be earnest and good," she told. "I find you both disappointing and unsurprising."

"He is Denny's brother," Jack said.

"I—well, I am hardworking. This—I—my mentor...it's complicated."

Violet crossed to him and lifted the knife. It was another of those wood and glass looking things. "This is a bad idea."

"I wasn't going to use it, I just—I—"

"Violet," Jack said, sounding exasperated. "Please get away from the criminal man with the knife."

"He's *Denny's* brother."

"Martha Dean was murdered by her husband and the father of her children, Violet. Step away."

Wendell paled, and he glanced between them. "I didn't—you don't understand."

"So explain," Violet said, hopping up on the desk next to Wendell. "Spill all your secrets, my lad."

"Violet," Jack snapped.

She turned and held out her hand. He sighed, crossing to her, pulling her from the desk and settling under his arm.

"He wouldn't do anything with you right here," Violet told Jack.

"I wouldn't do anything at all," Wendy shot back. "Never. You're Lila's dearest friend. She loves you more than her own sister."

"Lila is my dearest as well," Violet told him. "And she thinks you're earnest and hardworking. She went on about it. Makes me wonder if she wishes you were something that you're not."

Wendell closed his eyes. "I'm not the main archeologist. I'm one of the assistants. I just want to help Lands. He's a good man."

"That mentor you were talking about?" Jack asked.

Wendell was pale with bright circles of red on his cheeks. He nodded, and Violet glanced at Jack. His own gaze was focused on Wendell, but Violet wondered if he believed him.

"What are you looking for?" Jack asked.

"Greyly wanted Dr. Lands to claim he had found an obsidian dagger at our site. It wasn't even of the right era. And I'm not sure it wasn't a fake. Lands knows, and he's...well, he's been good to me. Greyly is obsessed with these obsidian blades, and they seem to be turning up all over the place in his digs. It's laughable, but Greyly just says whatever he wants and expects people to fall in line."

Violet sighed and handed Jack the knife. Jack glanced down at it and gave it back to Wendell.

"Why didn't you say any of this yesterday?"

"Are you kidding? Denny torments me on the best of days. He doesn't think I should want to work in Egypt digging up ancient *garbage,* and he generally disapproves of anything other than cock-tails, dancing, and his wife."

Violet shot Jack a look. He was far more calm about this revelation than Vi. Maybe she just wanted siblings to be something special. Violet frowned at Wendy. "You have a good brother."

"Are you serious?" Wendy demanded as Jack snorted.

Violet spun on Jack. "I like Denny!"

"I like Denny too, darling. But—his strengths don't seem to be the positives that you and I enjoy."

Vi stepped away from Wendy and Jack. "So what were you looking for?"

"Just what I was wondering," Jack added.

"Just proof. A letter, something. Something to give Lands a chance to clear his name from these interferences."

Violet lifted her brows, staring at him. "Or to destroy some supposed proof?"

"No, hardly that."

The reality was, Violet thought, they couldn't believe him. Greyly had Wendell under suspicions, and Vi suspected that any of these archeologists who'd been pulled into whatever this was called had reason to destroy evidence.

Violet glanced at Jack. "This Greyly is a scoundrel."

"So it seems," Jack said mildly.

"Why don't we help Wendell out of this...ah...scandalous employment?"

"How are you going to do that?" Wendell demanded. "I—no one will hire me now. I had no idea when—I appreciate your help, but Greyly is my life. I don't have another option, and working for Greyly is better than nothing."

Violet faced Jack. "You explain it. I've left my date."

He growled in his throat as she left them both. The night was wearing on, and she'd learned very little. It seemed to her that

Greyly was a scoundrel, that Lands and the rest had a good reason to despise the man, and that anyone who objected to the situation should have steeled his spine and left Greyly.

When Violet found her way back to the ballroom, Greyly cornered her. "I assume your Mr. Wakefield is working the case?"

"Mr. Wakefield can speak for himself. I, however, am bored." She grinned at him, took a cocktail from a passing tray, and made her way towards the cases again. The one with the jewelry was particularly interesting to her. Violet *loved* jewelry. She had a rather large amount of it, as she'd inherited from both her mother and great-aunt as well as been spoiled by her brother. Jack had taken up the mantle of spoiling Violet as well.

She ran her fingers over her gold bead necklace. The golden beads were the size of pearls, and they were strung in very long strands that was the fashion of the day. Her wrists were heavy with jewelry, and some time, centuries ago, another woman had lived and worn that heavy gold bracelet on the other side of the glass. Violet leaned closer to examine the etchings in the bracelet. It was just a simple etching, but it was lovely.

"Careful, sweet sister," Victor said. "If you lean too far over, you may just show the world the rest of your chest."

Violet straightened and spun on her brother. Her gaze flicked past him to Kate, who held a cocktail in one hand and Victor's arm in the other. "Hello, dear twin," Violet said smoothly. "Who knew that the same man who had to marry so swiftly would also be such a good guardian of my virtue?"

Kate burst into laughter as Victor blushed. "It has been entertaining to watch."

Violet bit back her smile to hide her humour. "Do you have the servants commanded to send for you should Jack appear?"

Victor's ears turned a bright red.

"And what about if you aren't there?"

Victor cleared his throat and glanced at Kate, who said, "Oh my love, I have nothing to do with this."

"Father controls my allowance," Victor told Violet as though she would accept such nonsense.

"I might find that more interesting," Violet told Victor, "if I weren't well aware of how much you have from Aunt Agatha."

"Trapped again," Kate told Victor, patting his chest. "Just tell her that your father is terrifying."

"That's not it," Violet told Kate.

"She should just stay my sister forever and never actually marry or move."

Kate rolled her eyes at Victor. "She's not going to stop being your twin. Quit being an idiot. She'll never find a man who puts up with you as well as Jack does."

"Jack won't go anywhere," Victor whined. "He knows he's won."

Violet sipped her cocktail to hide her grin. She had to admit—even if only to herself—that she was happy to see him as uncertain of what the future would hold without being in each other's pockets as she was.

CHAPTER NINE

*J*ack appeared when Violet left her brother for another cocktail. The party was moving from the ballroom towards the French doors, leading to the garden where servants had prepared the bonfire. The fire hadn't been lit yet, but the fireworks would be starting soon. There was a table covered with champagne glasses, and the area around the bonfire was lined with burning torches that were already lending a magical air to the outdoors. The heavy rain of earlier had ended, and they were lucky enough not to be caught in the wet as the evening festivities started.

Violet considered finding Parker and then decided against it. She saw Jack near Denny and Lila, and made her way towards them instead. She slipped her arm through Jack's and pressed her face into the warmth of him.

"I think we should stop with this fire investigation. Greyly should contact Scotland Yard and bring in official help rather than trying to manipulate you into helping him," she told him. "We should be spending our efforts on that other matter."

"What matter?" Victor demanded, but Violet only grinned evilly at her brother. His gaze sharpened on hers, but he couldn't know what they were up to so he wouldn't end up getting into trouble with his mother-in-law.

Jack shrugged. "We've been discussing our housing options."

"Just move into my house," Victor said.

Kate rolled her eyes behind Victor's shoulder, but Jack laughed and clapped Victor on the shoulder.

"I know you don't want Violet to move out, my friend, but she is going to all the same. I promise, however, that I won't drag her to Timbuktu with me."

Victor shuddered at that thought and then told Violet, "We're diving deep into a new series if you are moving out. That way you'll have to drop by all the time."

"Oh my goodness, you two are ridiculous," Kate said with a laugh. "Jack, the house at the end of the street is owned by a very old man who is finally moving in with his son. I suspect if you reached out to his man of business, you might be able to buy and renovate the house before you marry Violet. Vi, maybe renovating the house, writing your books, and managing your business interests will keep you out of trouble."

"Unlikely," Victor pronounced.

"On the very same street?" Violet demanded. She considered the houses in her mind. "The red one with the wrought iron fencing that is lilies?"

"No." Kate shook her head. "The grey stone one. His granddaughter and her children are there as well, but the house itself is owned by Mr. James, and they're all moving when Mr. James moves."

Violet paused without looking at Jack. She had become almost as stone-like as the house. That was her favourite house on the street, and its garden was even larger than Victor's. It was lovely. So close. She *wanted* it suddenly and deeply.

"I'll talk to them," Jack said, before Violet could even turn her gaze to his and let him see her thoughts. Maybe he could read them through the statue version of her, or maybe Victor's wide, wanting gaze was enough for both of them.

"Now you just need to buy a country house near Jack's family home," Violet said merrily, as Jack placed his hand over hers where it rested on his elbow. "And we'll be perfectly situated to stay in each other's pockets."

Victor nodded. "Shall we go country house shopping, Kate?"

She shook her head and told him, "We won't buy without looking this time."

Victor winced as the fireworks show began, and they all turned to watch the show. On the other side of the unlit bonfire, Denny and Lila were talking with Wendell and an older man that Violet hadn't met yet. He was almost as tanned as the Jones fellow from earlier, so Violet's guess was that was Dr. Lands, Wendell's mentor.

Denny lifted his champagne glass to her across the stack of wood. Jack waved over another servant, and they all took their glasses as another round of fireworks burst. There was a symphony playing in the background and the music wafted over the garden, adding to the festivities.

Violet took a deep breath, laying her head on Jack's shoulder. What if they were able to get that house? It *would* be perfect. She was afraid to get her hopes up. When they weren't surrounded by strangers, she'd need to make sure he knew she'd rather overpay than live farther away from her twin. She wasn't exactly sure of the state of Jack's affairs. She knew he wasn't poor and that he worked because he wanted to, but she wasn't sure if he had quite the same amount of capital as she had, given her inheritance.

Whatever it took, she thought, her attention being caught by a lovely burst of purple and blue. The torches were behind them, lighting the way back to the house, but the view in front of them was dark to let them see the fireworks clearly.

Small groups of shadows congregated here and there. Some of the women, like Vi, seemed to shimmer every time the fireworks exploded, but in general, it was impossible to say who was who now that they were away from the torches. Violet curled her fingers through Jack's and watched the show.

He was standing behind her, with his arms wrapped around her to keep her warm. She could feel the press of his chest against her head, and his chin settled on top of her head. "This could have been a better evening."

"I could have been your date," she told him. "Rather than poor Parker. I hope he doesn't mind that I abandoned him."

"Why him?"

"He's a legitimate archeologist."

"Then why is he here with the poseur and his table of minions?"

"Probably because I bribed him," Violet admitted.

The group oohed at a particularly large firework, and Violet felt his chuckle, though the sound of it didn't reach her.

When the gasps quieted, she said, "Perhaps a quiet dinner?"

"Then dancing?"

She started to agree, turning to face him, as a scream broke through the sounds of the fireworks and the music. Violet gasped, and Jack tugged her closer, instinctively protecting her from whatever had caused the scream. Shouts echoed the scream, and the lights on the back of the house went on.

"Before this begins," Jack told Violet, "You do look beautiful tonight."

Their gazes met. She could see the worry in his. Another fire?

Something else that would draw them back into this just as they were attempting to free themselves and focus on their own lives.

There was another scream that was followed by a deep shout, "Harvey! By Jove, it's Harvey! Send for a doctor." A moment later the command was followed with, "Now!"

"Stay here," Jack told Violet. "Whatever it is—you don't need to add it to your dreams."

She nodded, moving towards Victor and Kate. Injured or sick. Heart attack or even—please no—another murder, Violet had no desire to add to the fodder of her already excessively disturbing nightmares.

Violet placed her hand on her brother's elbow on the opposite side of Kate and then pressed up on her toes. There wasn't any way to see what was happening, but Violet tried all the same. She didn't want to see Greyly's injury or watch him expiring from a brain fever or something else, but her curiosity was burning.

Victor put his hand over her eyes. "Careful, love. No one enjoys to see our witty Vi stumble from those dreams of yours."

"He's dead," someone hissed.

Another person repeated it until it echoed from all sides like the wind in a storm. *Dead. Dead. Dead. Dead.*

"Do you think he had a heart attack or a brain attack?" Violet asked.

Victor paused. "He didn't look unhealthy."

Violet thought back. He really hadn't looked sick. But you didn't have to *look* sick to have something wrong inside. She wanted it to be a heart attack or some other natural cause. She wanted that so badly. It was a hard thing to believe with the fires. She glanced at Victor, who was thinking the same thing.

"The fires," he said.

"It would be rather a lot to believe it wasn't murder given the fires." Kate looked as sick and bothered at the idea as Violet felt.

There was a part of Violet that wanted to ask Jack to stay out of it.

If Greyly was dead and Jack was here, they'd get sucked into another investigation. Or Jack would. Violet would very definitely not be invited, and she wasn't sure she wanted to have anything to do with it. If her dreams were sending a message, they were telling her to stop getting involved with these murder cases.

Violet saw Denny and Lila moving through the crowd towards them. She nudged Victor and nodded towards their friends so they could move as a group over there. The crowd had moved towards the commotion, but Violet, Victor, and Kate had backed away. With Lila and Denny, there was quite the space between them and whatever Jack was having to deal with.

"What's happening?" Denny asked. He had his arm around Lila and was eyeing the people ahead of them as if they were animals. "We almost got trampled."

Violet shot them a disbelieving look and then caught Lila's expression in the light of the fire. Lila, who always seemed either bored or amused, looked harried.

"You all right, darling?" Violet asked. She let go of her brother for Lila and wrapped her arm around her friend so Lila was encapsulated between Denny and Violet.

Lila lied with a smile towards Violet, but she grabbed Denny's hand where it was on her waist. Violet could feel the clench of Lila's fingers into her husband's hand.

"Where's Wendy?" Victor asked. They all glanced around, looking for him.

"Maybe he's trying to help?" Kate suggested. She'd stepped into Victor's protection at the sight of Lila. "Was he with you?"

"He was," Denny said with a frown, looking behind him. He seemed to expect his brother to be right there. When he wasn't,

Denny searched through the crowd. It was too dark to see anything useful.

"When did he disappear?" Violet asked.

Denny's gaze settled on hers. It was dark, too dark to see the expression in each other's gaze, but Denny knew Violet well, and they all heard the edge of suspicion in her voice.

"Was it murder?" Lila demanded. "Even it was, it wasn't *Wendy*."

"All we know," Kate said carefully, "is that Harvey Greyly is dead."

Violet bit her lip. They knew quite a bit more than that, didn't they? They knew that someone was angry enough about what Greyly was doing that they were willing to commit arson. They knew that the men who worked for Greyly had their livelihoods on the line and had already put their working reputations at risk. Were any of them at greater risk of losing their reputation? Perhaps one of them *had* found something of great value. Something they didn't want to share with Greyly?

CHAPTER TEN

They were eventually escorted by the police into a parlor. The party had been split into groups as they went, and all of Greyly's archeologists were included in the parlor where Violet and her friends were placed.

"What's happening?" Lila whispered.

Violet's date, Parker, had joined Simon Jones across the room. They were in a pair of armchairs in a corner. Both had lit cigarettes and leaned back, smoking without conversation. Violet moved from them to the sofa across the room near the center of the room. It had the older man that Violet had noted before with Wendell Lancaster at his side. She also noted Wendell glancing their way, but he sat silently next to the man Violet assumed was the archeologist that Wendell had been working with.

There were a few other men in the room. Violet wondered if they were also associated with Harvey Greyly. She suspected that they were separated because they were more important to the case. Why were Violet and her friends here? Violet, Victor, and Kate—at least—could be alibied by Jack himself. Violet had little doubt that Lila and Denny were here because of their link to Wendell Lancaster and his link to the dead man.

Violet took a seat next to Kate, laying her head on Kate's shoulder. "What do you think, Kate? Are we dealing with murder?"

"I would expect so," Kate murmured. "Otherwise we wouldn't have been segregated like this."

Violet shuddered. She was so *tired* of stumbling over bodies and murderers. How hard was it to *not* kill your enemies? How hard was it to make other changes in your life rather than to slaughter someone in your way?

Violet glanced down at Kate's stomach and considered Violet Junior, who was growing. They fought so hard during the Great War to preserve this way of life. For what? To bring little ones into the world to be slaughtered in their own homes instead of in the trenches?

"Take that look off of your face," Victor told her, reaching out and grabbing her hand. "Stop thinking so hard about this."

"Why shouldn't I think hard about it?" she asked him, drawing her hand away and clasping both together. "Why aren't you thinking hard about it? Why aren't you bothered?"

"Darling Vi," Victor said. "People have killed each other over stupid stuff since Cain and Abel. Yet, siblings have also been like we are. Has our life been so hard that we shouldn't have existed?"

Violet shook her head. She dug her fingers into her wrist where she was grasping her hand, and shook her head again. This was the melancholy coming on again, she thought. She needed to move. To breathe, to distract herself.

She rose and crossed to Wendy before she could think about it too long and settled next to him. "Wendy!"

"It's Wendell," he replied, sounding exhausted.

"Tell me a story," she begged. "I'm thinking sad thoughts. Did you see what happened?"

Wendy's gaze fixed on Violet, so like Denny's, and he shook his head.

"It wasn't an accident. Not with us having been ushered into here."

"I'm afraid not, my dear," the older man said. "I'm Dr. Lands. I'd say it was a pleasure, but it feels a bit unkind to make such a statement."

"Lady Violet Carlyle," Vi replied. "I am delighted to meet the man who has mentored my friend's younger brother. I only wish it were under better circumstances. I fear my own brother still looks at Wendy and sees the boy who used to muck about in the garden. Imagine! Making that your life."

"It's Wendell," Wendy said.

Vi smiled at him, patting his hand.

"And you also, Dr. Lands, work uncovering hidden treasures in the garden. Sort of like you're mucking about but with more purpose these days."

"Ah, yes. Well, I suppose we do."

Violet fluttered her lashes prettily at him and asked, "How do you determine where to dig?"

Dr. Lands flushed a little. "It's a combination of rumors, other digs, theories of my own—or at times others..."

"Others like Mr. Greyly?"

Dr. Lands's flush intensified and he nodded. "Yes."

Violet could see it was a point of contention. Wendell shifted with that look on his face that would have said Denny had stolen the chocolates you were looking for. On Wendell, Violet suspected it meant that he knew what was making Dr. Lands uncomfortable but wouldn't be sharing.

Violet ignored both of their discomfort as she asked, "And

where have you been digging?"

Dr. Lands frowned. "We've been having quite an unsuccessful dig, I fear."

Had they really? That did lessen him as the perpetrator of the fire assuming the fires had been set to destroy something that had been found on one of the digs or perhaps something associated with that the archeologists had been doing. She felt the fires and the murder rather had to be linked. "What about these others? Where have they been working? Somewhere exotic and wonderful?"

"Simon Jones has been working for some time in Greece," Dr. Lands said. "These things can take years to do properly."

"But that isn't what Mr. Greyly really cared about was it? Working carefully?"

Dr. Lands glanced sharply at Violet, who said, "I fear my companion this evening was not much of a fan of Mr. Greyly. I came with Henry Parker."

Dr. Lands lifted his brows. "I saw him. I was rather surprised he was invited."

"The invitation was extended to me," Violet told Dr. Lands. "I met Dr. Parker at the British Museum and asked him to come and explain what I was seeing here."

"I can't imagine he had very many good things to say about the work Mr. Greyly was financing. I've heard his opinion." Dr. Lands's expression was fierce, and Violet felt a flash of alarm.

"People can have differing opinions about a subject and both have a relatively reasonable standpoint? I can only imagine that the fellow who found Troy he was quite mocked by some."

"Yes, I imagine so."

"So, where were these others digging?"

"There are two other main archeologists who work—ah, worked—for Greyly. Jones and Richard Lovegood worked in

Greece. I worked in part of Egypt. The one we haven't discussed is George Morgan, who has been working on one of those tiny islands in the Aegean Sea."

"Oh, he hasn't been mentioned yet. Tell me about him."

"I don't know him all that well," Dr. Lands said, as the door to the parlor opened and Jack stepped in.

"I apologize for keeping all of you here," Jack announced. "For those who didn't see or know, our host, Harvey Greyly, has died."

"Who are you?" Simon Jones asked loudly. "And why are we being kept here?"

Violet's eyes tried to narrow, but she kept them bright and wide as she looked at Simon Jones. Her thoughts were hid behind her expression, and she hoped she seemed rather like a girl looking for a gossip rather than anything else.

"The nature of Greyly's death makes it clear that he was murdered," Jack said.

Not one person gasped except for Jones, who blustered. "Well how did he die?"

Violet was having a very hard time believing that someone in this room hadn't seen the body already and that Jones hadn't gotten that information from the person himself. Why was he pretending to be so shocked?

"He was stabbed," Jack said clearly. "We will speak with each of you one by one. We'll take your information for the case to continue."

"Why are *you* investigating? Where are the real police?"

Jack's face was unmoved as he spoke to the room at large. "It is true that I am a sometime investigator for Scotland Yard, but my assistance has been requested in this case. Make yourself comfortable. I fear this will take rather longer than we'd all prefer. Mrs. Carlyle, I'll take you and Mr. Carlyle first."

Violet started, wondering who he meant before the realization that Kate had become Mrs. Carlyle settled in. It was too new for it to be comfortable for any of them, but Victor had married, Kate had become Mrs. Carlyle, and they'd even have a baby soon. Violet tried to keep the surreal madness from her face as she watched her twin and sister-in-law leave. Victor glanced back at her with a silent command to be careful and shake the blues that were threatening.

Violet's state of mind was definitely askew with what'd she'd been through since the murder of her great aunt, but she'd also met Kate and Jack in that time frame. They were, Violet reminded herself, worth any matter of trials, and the sheer fact that she and her twin had fallen in love showed that the world was a beautiful place as well.

Violet focused on the beauty of it even as she leaned back and said, "By Jove! Can it be murder?"

"I fear a stabbing makes it so, my dear," Dr. Lands said. Violet slowly turned. It had been a rhetorical question, but he didn't know her well enough to know why she was baffled. She would have preferred a terrible illness or horrific accident than the deliberate coldness of a slaying.

"Lady Violet," Wendy told his mentor, "and her friends have solved rather a number of murder cases."

"And yet you are baffled by this one?" Dr. Lands's scoff was deserved, Violet thought. A bright young thing in a flashy dress and her friends, and they'd solved crimes? It was hard to believe when her makeup didn't feel smeared.

"I am endlessly baffled by the cruelties of humanity. Take this murder," Violet said. "The man who was killed tonight was the patron of each of you. He made your work possible—a work that Wendy," Violet ignored his wince, "as well as Dr. Parker has explained is difficult to do without a man like Greyly to step in and donate his own funds to pay the way."

Dr. Lands glanced around the room.

"Greyly's digs have something of a reputation," Violet told Lands bluntly. "So it's rather farfetched to believe that any of you will ever work again."

Lands cleared his throat. "That's rather succinct."

"And unkind," Violet agreed.

"But true," Land sighed. "Quite true, I'm afraid."

"Were you with anyone during the fireworks show?" Violet asked him.

He smiled at her as he replied. "Surely people will lie to you with these answers. How do you find the truth?"

"Rather like you, I suspect," Violet said mildly. "Investigators like Jack patch together evidence and follow it. Maybe we'll be lucky and someone will have blood on their shoes and no alibi, and we can all go home."

"Unlikely," Lands shot back.

"Agreed," Violet said. "You're all educated men. Anyone planning a murder isn't going to be ruined by something as easy as blood on their clothes."

Violet glanced down Lands. His shoes were perfect. Shining. They looked as though they'd never been worn. She glanced to Wendy, whose shoes were ones she'd seen on Denny time and again. They were a bit loose on Wendy, but they were clean. As a group, they leaned over and examined the shoes of the man who was sitting across the way.

Nothing to see there or across the room on Jones and Parker even though they were too distant to truly tell.

"If he doesn't find someone with their shoes or some blood on their pants, what will he do next?"

"They'll figure out where everyone was—start ruling them out —and then focus on those who don't have a witness for their location during the murder. He'll string together clues and narrow in on a person or two and then find the evidence to exonerate or trap the man."

"A woman could have stabbed Greyly," Lands reminded Violet. "If history has taught us anything it is that women are treacherous."

"Yet not as treacherous as men," Violet said. "Unless you have a woman working one of these digs, it was one of you who killed Greyly."

"Why one of us?"

Violet lifted a brow at Wendell and waited to see if he'd answer. He did a moment later.

"Because, Stephen, who else but one of us would have been setting those fires? It's a bit of a stretch to believe we're all back in the country at Greyly's request, the fires start surrounding the work we've done, and then he comes up dead. If someone killed Greyly, it has to be at least associated with the fires, doesn't it? Maybe it was someone protecting the arsonist, maybe it was the arsonist who killed Greyly, but what did you teach me? You follow the clues of the past, you follow your instincts, but you make sure that a rational mind is involved as well. People didn't build villages at the worst possible locations in a valley unless there was a reason."

"And murderers have a reason as well." Violet's gaze flicked around the room, taking in each of the men who had been involved in Greyly's work. "The reason doesn't have to be one that makes sense to the world at large, but there is always a reason for why someone kills another. Clues, instinct, and reason. Jack will follow those to find the killer. Maybe along the way, he'll uncover some hidden crime of Greyly that will take the focus off of the men who worked for him. But right now, all reason and all instinct and all clues say it was one of you."

CHAPTER ELEVEN

*O*ne of the uniformed officers stepped into the room and stood in front of the door. He didn't move and he didn't speak.

"Are we being held captive, my good man?" Jones asked, running his hand over his thick pelt of hair. His eyes were tight as he glanced around the room. "What is happening?"

The police officer's gaze landed on Violet for a moment before he turned to Jones and said, "Nothing like that, sir. Nothing like that." He didn't move, however, from in front of the door.

Violet played with the ring on her finger as she glanced around the room. It was telling, she thought, that Jack hadn't pulled Violet with Victor and Kate, and yet there was a police officer in the room. Was he telling her to find out what she could while also ensuring she was safe? She had little doubt that Jack would make it clear if he didn't like what she was up to, so she turned her gaze back to Wendell. "You were with Denny and Lila when the fireworks started, but you left sometime during the show."

Wendy sniffed and then asked, "How do you know that?"

"When the screaming started your brother and his wife made their way to my brother and me. They thought you were behind them."

Dr. Lands glanced at the younger archeologist, and his brows rose. There was something in his face that made Violet wonder if he knew where Wendell had gone.

"Maybe I just went to see what was happening?"

"What are you answering that like a question?"

"Why are you asking? You were asked to look into the fires, but we both know that Greyly really wanted your fiancé, not you."

"Your patron is dead," Violet shot back. She glanced up when she saw movement out of the corner of her eye and found Lila and Denny seat themselves in the nearest chairs.

"Why are you avoiding the question, old man?" Denny asked his brother.

"Your friend thinks I killed Greyly."

"Vi doesn't think that," Denny told his younger brother lazily. "She knows me too well."

Wendell scoffed and shot back, "Just because you are too lazy to kill someone doesn't mean I am."

"Oh." Violet followed Wendell's gaze to Denny. That statement had been filled with fury. "Why are you angry with your brother?"

Wendy turned to Violet. "He wastes himself and his brains. He spends his days drinking and eating. He's fat because he doesn't move."

"Fat is going a bit far, I'd say," Lila mused. "More, ah, a bit chubby."

"He wouldn't last a day in my life." Wendell clenched his fists and spoke through his gritted teeth.

"Well, who would want to?" Denny asked reasonably, keeping his lazy tone in the face of his brother's fury. Violet noted that Denny wasn't all that surprised by the anger from his brother. Was this a family fight they'd had time and again? She guessed it was, but what surprised her was that Denny so accepting.

"Our aunt should never have left the money to you."

"Oh ho," Violet breathed to Lila, who shrugged. Denny just crossed his legs and leaned back. Again, neither of them were surprised.

Wendell shot a glance to Violet and snapped, "Am I wrong? You know them better than I do, you think? Hardly. Are you aware of how lazy they are? How they spend their days doing *nothing?*"

"I suspect that I know Denny and Lila *quite* a bit better than you do," Violet told him smoothly. She adjusted her necklace and then spun her ring. "Shall I make a guess then?"

Wendell shot her a nasty glance while Denny waved her on.

"Your aunt left the money to Denny rather than *you* because she wanted to support the coming generation and not a dig in some distant part of the world."

Denny gave Violet the very slightest of nods.

"What generation?" Wendell demanded. "Lila and Denny have been married for years. Where are the children? It was all for nothing."

"Perhaps the chance of children was worth more than the guarantee that you'd spend your life not having children, creating a family, or moving the family generations forward."

Wendell flushed.

"Jealousy doesn't become you," Violet told him flatly. "Especially given how I've heard these two talk about you."

OBSIDIAN MURDER

Dr. Lands cleared his throat and placed a hand on Wendell's shoulder.

"Do you know what Lila told me when I was asked to help? That you were earnest and hardworking. They're proud of you."

Wendell flushed brilliantly and his glance towards Denny was uncomfortable for everyone who saw it.

"Let's set aside the fighting and you can tell me why you didn't kill Greyly."

Wendell grounded his teeth. "You don't understand what it's like to see your dreams snatched away!"

"I probably understand better than anyone else how this could have happened. I was also the greater inheritor. Victor is rich enough from Aunt Agatha. My cousins who inherited got *significantly* less money. Do you want to know how you *should* have reacted? I can introduce you to them, and you can learn proper behavior from my family. Tell me where you were when Greyly was killed."

Wendell thrust himself to his feet, saw the police officer, and sat back down.

"Why don't we avoid who got the money and focus on who the killer is?" Violet suggested.

"You think I'm just going to let you trap me into confessing? I didn't kill the man."

"Honestly," Violet told him flatly, "your behavior makes you incredibly suspicious. However, I value the opinion of your brother and his wife, and they're convinced you didn't do it. Let's assume you didn't, and you tell me where you were so we can narrow down who did it, and you can go back to being jealous of your brother's money."

Wendell flushed. "I wrote an article to Greyly's specifications. Dr. Lands told me to take it back, but Greyly wouldn't give it to me. He owns the journal that publishes the nonsense we write for him.

He refused to return it. He refused to remove my name from it. He intended to ruin my career. I was just trying to find it. He hadn't had a chance to send it off yet. He shouldn't have anyway. I—"

Violet glanced at Dr. Lands, who seemed unsurprised. Why was he so accepting of his protégé digging through the offices of his patron? "Were you together?"

Wendell glanced at Lands and shook his head. "Ah, no. I hadn't found what I needed earlier when you found me, so I took the chance to search again during the fireworks. I know it was wrong, but...by Jove, so was what Greyly was doing to us."

Violet hid her reaction to that rush of fury and looked to the mentor. "Where were you, Dr. Lands?"

"Just in the crowd," he said without hesitation. Was it because that was the truth or because he had an answer prepared?

"I understand you intend to publish a book to counteract the damage you've done working for Greyly?"

Dr. Lands's brows rose and he admitted, "That wasn't well known."

"Parker told me," Violet admitted.

Dr. Lands eyed Violet. "I'm surprised my old friend would tell you that."

"I bribed him," Violet told him bluntly. She glanced towards Parker, who met her gaze. She didn't know him well enough to know how he'd feel about her revelation, but if she had to guess, her guess would be that he'd shrug at Lands and tell him that patrons were hard to find and the work was important.

"Why?" Wendell demanded.

"Denny and Lila love you. If you're important to them, you're important to me."

The flush of anger changed, and his entire face was brilliantly red. "I—"

"Don't worry about it, Wendell," Denny told his brother. "Help Violet help you. Did anyone see you when you were digging through Greyly's stuff for your article?"

"I was trying to not be seen." Wendell's jaw gritted. "I'm—" His tone reflected the desire to apologize, but he didn't quite get it out.

"Why did Greyly come to you about the fires?" Dr. Lands asked Violet.

She sighed and leaned back. "Sometimes I've meddled. Sometimes it helped to find killers. The real reason, however, is that Jack Wakefield is a famous investigator."

"Who's Jack Wakefield?"

"He's my intended," Violet said. "We'll be married in April. Greyly manipulated all of us. He heard about Jack through my father. He had issues with fires. He wanted the arsonist found, and he used Denny and Wendell to get to me."

"You aren't with Jack Wakefield." Dr. Lands glanced Violet over, lingering on the dip in her dress over her chest.

"I've been hurt a few times while I've meddled."

"So Greyly got you involved to get your fiancé involved?"

Why had she let herself get sucked into this? She remembered that feeling of melancholy and realized that it was her own state of mind that had pulled her into this. The intrigue had faded her blues. She needed to find another way to deal with these flashes of emotion.

"I am thinking so." Violet took a deep breath in. "Manipulated on all sides. It's a real blow to my pride."

"What do you do, Lady Violet, when you aren't meddling?"

Violet's head tilted as she examined Dr. Lands. "I write books, manage investments, enjoy dancing, cocktails, and time with the people I love. I take my dog for walks and sometimes I spend the day lazing about my bedroom doing nothing at all. I have the luxury of doing whatever I wish."

"Wouldn't that be nice?" Dr. Lands asked Wendell. "To not have to worry about money, and you could do whatever you wanted?"

"It is nice," Denny told them.

"Wendy is doing what he wants," Lila snapped. "He has wanted to dig up ancient worlds since he was a grubby little boy. You can tell yourself these woeful tales, but he isn't suffering like Denny did in those offices."

"Oh, poor Denny," Wendell shot back. "He was educated as well as I was, and he had the options to go to whatever school he wanted and get whatever education he needed for whatever career."

Lila's eyes narrowed on Wendell. "He got the education he needed to support us, you idiot. Your aunt didn't owe either of you the money. She left it to Denny because you were happy and he was miserable. Because you have no desire for a family and Denny and I do. She left it where she *wanted,* which was her right."

Wendell met Lila's gaze, who didn't flinch in the slightest. They two of them stared each other down. Denny started to speak, but Violet grabbed his arm. It was Lila's right to defend her husband and Wendell deserved it even if they'd help him regardless.

"You're right," he finally said. "I was wrong. I was always wrong. I even knew it. I told Dr. Lands about it, and he said the same thing. It was her money to do with as she wanted. It was done, and I should let it go. To be happy for you. I am. I know Denny hated that job. Bloody hell! I—Denny—"

"I'd have been jealous too," Denny told Wendell. "Never

thought she'd give it to me. Everyone knows you worked way harder than I did."

CHAPTER TWELVE

$\mathcal{J}$ack came back into the room and waved Violet into a corner.

"What have you found out?" Jack's gaze flicked down Violet, and he handed her the wrap that Kate had been wearing. "She thought you might want it."

Violet did want the wrap. She didn't object to her dress. She had worn it on purpose when she wanted to take a slew of archeologists by surprise and flirt answers from them about possible arson. As one of two women in a room full of possible killers, she definitely didn't want their attention. Violet wrapped it around her shoulders and shimmied a little as she glanced up at Jack through her lashes.

"Wendy was looking for the article he wrote for Greyly when the killing happened. He doesn't have any witnesses to where he was. It turns out that Dr. Lands advised Wendy not to put his name to one of Greyly's articles. I think that Lands regrets his life working for Greyly and was trying to help Wendy."

Jack nodded. "Digging through the dead man's things during

the murder is hardly a good alibi. I have to admit, however, that from what I've been able to discover, Wendell had every reason to be concerned about Greyly's intentions. What about Lands?"

"He says he was in the crowd. I'm not sure what to believe there. I wouldn't be surprised if he was trying to help Wendell."

Jack looked Violet over again. "Are you all right?"

She nodded.

"Did you see the body?"

Violet shook her head.

"If we wrap this up quickly, do you think you'll have those dreams?"

Violet paused before answering. "I have no idea. I'm trying, Jack. I don't want to have nightmares or get the blues. I'm sorry." She looked down, hating this feeling. It was like she was unworthy of his caring.

"Violet Carlyle," Jack snapped. "You don't get to slide out of loving me or escape the life we're crafting. So I suggest that you help me find this killer and then we'll go home. We'll have dinner the next day at the Savoy, we'll go for a walk along the river, and we'll find a way. You've said yes, and I'm not letting you go."

"I don't want to go. I want that house," Violet shot back. "I want to *eventually* have your children, but maybe not right away. I want to wake up from my nightmares and know you'll be there, and I want to marry you. I just...feel like you can do better than me."

Violet had no doubt that if they didn't have an audience of murder suspects he'd press a kiss on her forehead and then move down her face. His gaze was burning, and it promised that when the chance appeared, he'd make those kisses happen.

"Who do you think killed him?"

Violet took a deep breath in and faced the room. Everyone was fixated on the two of them and not one of them looked upset or guilt-ridden. She looked back to Jack, who said, "It could be any of them, Violet."

"Victor took Kate home?"

"Even I've heard her sicking up, Violet. I wasn't going to make her stay when I knew she didn't have anything to do with this case or the people involved. Victor made me promise not to let you leave without me. I'd like to keep you."

"Do you have faith in my ability to help?"

"I've never not had that faith, Vi," Jack said. "If it were a different time, you would be a good investigator. I prefer the present time when I know you're a little safer."

Violet grinned and whispered, "Real police officers have to work every day and don't get to take naps."

"That's true," Jack said. "I can't remember my last nap."

"It was in Cuba. Or by the sea. You definitely napped."

"Does it count if you're snoozing in a chair?"

"Those are just man-naps." Violet laughed behind her hand, hiding her humour from the room. "Shall we go somewhere warm, and you can nap in a chair there?"

"Yes," Jack said. "Greece?"

"I don't care where," Violet said. "I sleep better when I can hear the sea."

"We should consider a seaside cottage," Jack said. "After we get the house in London."

"I have a lot of capital," Violet told him. "These houses are for both of us and whatever children we end up having."

"I have enough for the house, Violet." Jack grinned for a moment and then asked, "How long were you fighting with how to offer the money?"

"Since the second I heard of it, so not long. I'd rather overpay drastically, Jack, than live farther away from Vi Junior."

"Let alone your twin." Jack took her hand and squeezed her

fingers. "I'll have my man over in the morning. I've already made a note. That house is my priority, even over this case. Ham is on his way. I asked them to send him quickly. He'll be here and accompanying you with this side of things, but not as an actual investigator. He'll be playing the overprotective friend. On purpose, so don't let it assault your modern woman."

Violet's head cocked, and she winked at Jack since they had an audience.

"I'm going to delay asking further questions by clearing the people who were here as random guests. I want to give you and Ham time to work the room. Violet, don't leave with anyone other than Ham, myself, or Denny. That includes young Wendell."

Violet nodded. She didn't want to be hurt again. It had taken far too long to get over her injuries last Christmas. She had a wedding to avoid planning, a house of her own to purchase and decorate, and a life to live. Just because she'd been lucky before and survived, did not mean she'd be lucky again.

"Victor is sending a babysitter," Violet told Denny and Lila as she rejoined them. "He doesn't want anything to happen to me when he takes Kate home, so I'll be watched over by our good friend, Hamilton Barnes."

Denny froze for a moment. "Ham, you say. Good man." He didn't refer to anything about Barnes's position as a commander at Scotland Yard. Barnes's intent to go incognito among the group would hopefully help them find the killer more quickly. At least, that was her hope.

"Surely your fiancé will clear you and send you home," Dr. Lands said. "No need for you to stay. It's one thing for Greyly to get you involved and another thing for your man to keep you involved."

Violet nibbled her bottom lip. "I might have seen something

that he'll need to know more about later. You never know. It's one thing to send home the people who clearly weren't involved, but I fear I was more involved in this case than I should have been to be able to slide out and go home to my bed without a conversation about what I might have witnessed." Violet touched Lila's shoulder. "I'm going to go apologize to Parker for leaving him on the dance floor."

Wendy snorted, but Violet ignored him and crossed to the corner where Jones and Parker were watching the rest of the room.

"Come to torture the truth out of us?" Jones asked. "I hear you're a wiseacre when it comes to trapping fellows into confessions."

"Who me?" Violet asked, leaning against the wall near them. She played with the ring on her finger and said, "Parker's in the clear. Mostly." Violet smirked at the little man, whose gaze widened behind his glasses. "The police will add what he saw to the list of facts and details, especially since he doesn't have much of a reason to kill Greyly."

"I don't know about that," Jones said, grinning at Parker. "He cares more about the integrity of the community more than anything else. I think Parker might have the strongest motive for killing Greyly than all of us."

Parker flushed brilliantly as he stuttered. Violet felt a flash of sympathy at the sight of his face. "You know what I find telling? No one in here is upset. Greyly was the patron of four of these men and their underlings. People could be losing their life's work."

Jones leaned back, crossing his leg. "We've already lost it. It's been a long, slow decline and all that is left is the burial we all knew was coming. You know what's the worst of it? Greyly has been hinting around that he might be done anyway. Pulling us all in, one final hurrah, and then he'd cut us loose."

Violet hid the shock on her face. *Bloody hell!* Did the archeologists know? What if they lost their last chance to pursue this work? What would they have done then if they'd known? Violet took a deep breath in and then let it slowly out, trying to hide her reaction. What kind of madness was this?

She asked Parker, "Would you introduce me to Richard Lovegood?"

Parker nodded, his gaze resting on Jones. "What are you going to do next, my old friend?"

"I'll find something, Parker. Don't you worry."

Violet turned to Jones. "Did you have a retirement plan before Greyly died?"

He nodded. "I've been saving since I realized that teaching or lecturing wasn't going to happen for me. I've been thinking about a little pub on the sea. Not in England, somewhere warm."

Violet could understand that sentiment. She wanted to be somewhere warm very much. It was past time she thought to head to the Amalfi Coast and spend some time in the house that Aunt Agatha left her. She fiddled with her ring before Parker stood and held out his arm. As he did, Hamilton Barnes entered the room in a brown suit. His cheeks were a little ruddy. If Vi had to guess, he'd been drinking wherever he'd been celebrating the evening.

"I'm sorry you had to leave whatever you were doing," she said when she joined her and Parker.

"I'm not, love." Ham grinned at Violet. "Emily Allen was there. She was wondering what Jack was up to and whether he'd left you yet. She feels certain it's just a matter of time before you're left behind, and he's a free agent again."

"So she'll be ready to rescue him from bachelorhood?"

"Just so, my dear," he told Violet. "She doesn't realize that Jack is fully shackled to you."

"Shackled!" Violet glanced at Parker and Jones. "Can you believe this nonsense?"

"Yes," Parker said, nodding frantically, "that seems the likeliest."

"Gentlemen," Violet said with a frown. "May I introduce my keeper, Ham Barnes? My brother sent him to keep the killer from slaughtering me too."

Ham's gaze twinkled at Violet as he bowed slightly at her introduction.

"I would wish you luck," Parker told Ham, "but I doubt anyone could keep her out of trouble. Did you know she showed up at my work, bribed me, and made a date with me?"

"Sounds like Vi," Ham agreed, holding out a hand to Jones. "Nice to meet you."

"And you," Dr. Jones replied. He glanced around the room and then looked to Barnes. "Do you think that you can keep her out of trouble?"

Ham laughed and shook his head. "No one could. Her twin is protective. Tell me, Jones, if you were to guess who the killer is—who do you think did it?"

Jones glanced at Parker and demanded, "Are we leaving Parker out of it?"

"Just for now," Barnes said. They didn't know that Barnes was a Scotland Yard man, Jack's boss, and Jack's commanding officer during the Great War when both Jack and Hamilton were part of the military police. Barnes was playing his part as a friend at the moment, and he was letting Jack take lead while he was in disguise as Violet's keeper.

"I don't know really," Jones said. "Lovegood isn't that far from retiring. I'm not sure why he'd be driven to fires and murder after all this time—that goes for all of us, doesn't it? The one who has the most to lose is your friend Wendell."

Violet's mouth twisted at that idea. She glances at Barnes, who didn't seem surprised at the answer. How many times had Barnes heard accusations thrown about and how did he handle it without turning a hair? "Parker was just going to introduce us to Lovegood," she told Barnes. "I haven't met him yet."

"I wonder how reasonable it is to think that the new man on the job is the killer," Violet said, as they moved across the room.

"I would imagine that it's easier to believe a stranger is a killer than a person you've known for years," Barnes answered.

"But," Violet whispered, "they're all working on different sites, aren't they? How close of friends could they be?"

The final group of people in the room was an older archeologist, defined by his tanned face and neck and his thick shoulders, another who was a younger version of the older man, and a very, very slim man who was almost ghostly pale.

"May I introduce Richard Lovegood, his nephew, James Lovegood, and Mr. Lyle Clarkson."

Parker introduced Violet without explaining that she had been used to draw Jack into the arson cases.

"Now," Violet said to the two Lovegoods, "you worked one of the Greece digs?"

Richard Lovegood nodded.

"Did you also find one of the obsidian knives?"

He focused on Violet for a moment and then shook his head. "I believe that you mean the knives Greyly sent to us to support his wild theories? They're not even worth repeating now that Greyly is gone. It was laughable in the extreme."

"Now, now," Clarkson squeaked. "We shouldn't speak ill of the dead."

Violet placed her hand on Clarkson and said, "May I ask how you're connected to Greyly?"

He paled even further before he answered, "I was his assistant."

"You're more than that, my boy," Lovegood told Clarkson, who flushed.

"And his nephew."

"And his heir," Lovegood finished.

The pale man flushed, and he repeated in a near whisper, "And Uncle Greyly's heir."

"The one," Lovegood added loudly, "who had the greatest reason to murder the old man."

"I—" Clarkson lost the flush and turned a sickly greenish white, and then he fainted.

CHAPTER THIRTEEN

*V*iolet stared down at the man at her feet and then glanced at Barnes, who leaned down and checked his pulse.

"Do you have smelling salts?" the younger Lovegood asked Violet.

"Smelling salts?" Violet demanded. "What am I? Your grandmother?"

They had been surrounded after Clarkson hit the ground, and Denny replied calmly, "If only he could be so lucky."

Jack and several police officers rushed into the room with another man following after with a doctor's bag. Jack pulled Violet behind him as though she were in danger. "What happened?"

"He fainted," Barnes told Jack.

"Did something happen to make him faint?"

"He's Greyly's heir," Barnes replied with a sigh. "He didn't look well before he fainted."

"Violet, Barnes, go into the hall," Jack said. "The rest of you move to the parlor across the hall. Leave the doctor to work on this man."

Jack joined them shortly after the rest of the crowd had moved into the parlor. He pulled Violet into the office they'd seen before and sent out the police officer who was searching the room. "We found Wendell's article," Jack told Violet. "Even I can identify it as nonsense. Something about trading of the obsidian blades to support worship of Hephaestus and a cult. Vi, it's *ridiculous*."

Violet pressed her forehead against Jack's chest. "This is the dumbest evening I've ever been part of," Violet told Jack. "Except there's a dead man."

"It would have ruined Wendell Lancaster's career, that article. This Greyly was trying to prove ghosts were real as well. He has been paying quite a sum of money towards mediums and spiritualists as well as these digs. He was obsessed with the Greek god of volcanoes, with the afterlife, with making a name for himself in sharing his obsessions and trying to have them widely accepted."

Violet looked up at Jack. "I understand why Clarkson would want to kill Greyly if he thought Greyly was throwing his money away. I *understand* it," Violet said. "I just *understand* it. Understand?"

Jack kissed her forehead. "Yes. You'd never even consider such a crime and it makes you sick to your heart, but you see how others think that way. Have you seen the inside of the grey stone house?"

Violet shook her head. "Only the outside. Does it matter?"

"You only care that it's at the end of the street where Victor lives?"

"And Vi junior. Do you care that we haven't seen it?"

"Violet," Jack said, "I don't care at all. But I have been wondering if by not caring, we're...being irresponsible."

Violet took a deep breath. "I don't know that I care, and we can afford to be irresponsible. Maybe we're being emotional about where we live. Maybe in choosing to live there instead of somewhere else, we're paying some sort of emotional tax. Surely, the price we pay for the things we want—that bring us happiness —are worth paying a higher price."

"I think so. I find that Greyly hauling us into these arsons has made me far more likely to care less about this case. Or maybe it was that in seeing the last victim's family and how broken they were, this is empty by comparison. No one cares that Greyly died," Jack told Violet, sounding more bothered by that than by the death of Greyly. "I think that's even sadder than the poor woman's children being left as orphans. Can you imagine? Dying and no one even caring?"

Violet shook her head.

"Violet Carlyle soon to be Wakefield?"

"Yes?" she asked him, as he wrapped his arms around her and hugged her close.

"I would be devastated if something happened to you."

"And I you," she said against his chest, not understanding why he needed to say it to her right then, but she knew he needed to know she loved him.

"It turns out that truly being in love and loving gives life meaning. What is the meaning to Greyly's life? He was looking for life's meaning in all these projects. The futile pursuits of ghosts and Hephaestus?"

"You think that matters?" she asked.

"I think that someone's life's meaning is or was at risk. A duel between what Greyly wanted and what the killer wanted."

Violet pulled away, hopping up onto the desk again. She held up her hand and ticked off names as she said them. "Wendell, Lands, Lovegood the elder, Lovegood the younger, Jones,

Clarkson. They all were mucked up in Greyly's life. He pulled them in with his money, tangled up in his theories and madness. No one liked him; they liked his money. Do I do the same thing?"

Jack shot Violet a look that told her she was ridiculous. She sighed. "I bribed Parker."

"For Wendell, because you love Lila and Denny."

"He just needs a chance," Violet said. "We could give him one and then he can do with it as he pleases. If he fails with the chance we give him, it's on Wendell. It will no longer matter that Denny got the inheritance instead of Wendell."

"What now?"

"Turns out earnest, hardworking Wendy is also a bit jealous."

"Of *Denny?*"

"The money from the aunt. It feels...familiar."

Jack shook his head. "Victor didn't mind that you got more money than he did."

"What about Algie and Davies? My cousins had every right to expect more from Aunt Agatha or as much as I got."

"That's not how inheritance works, Vi. Especially from an aunt. I could see someone being upset if they didn't inherit more evenly from a parent. But an aunt? No one has a right to look at an aunt and think that money should be mine."

Violet nodded. "How long are you going to keep them?"

"Not one of them was in the view of any of the guests," Jack told Violet. "No one who was watching the fireworks noticed them. Where were they?"

"The Lovegoods might alibi each other. It's not a stretch to assume they were together."

"Yet it's also not a stretch to assume that they would lie for each other."

"Maybe they were all in on it."

"That would make a good book. The average person would never consider killing someone else."

Violet glanced around the office. The walls were covered with pictures from digs and discoveries. There were empty spots where the police officers had removed photographs from the wall in order to show them to those they'd interviewed, verifying the suspects location during the party. There were framed coins and pictures of digs. There was an imaginative painting of the sphinx with the sun in the background. It didn't look like it was in modern times but what it might have been like when it was completed.

Violet loved the painting, and it made her want to see it desperately, but it lent nothing to the moment.

"Jack, maybe we should go and leave it to another investigator. Simply move on with the things that matter to us?"

"This does matter to me. I am offended by myself," he told her. "That I care less about Greyly than I should. Perhaps it would be good to break after the last case, but first, we need to do what we can to find Greyly's killer."

There was a knock on the door, and Barnes came into the room. "Nothing?" Ham asked.

Jack shook his head. "No one saw anything. The servants were preparing warmed cocktails. They weren't in the ballroom nor were they watching the show. Greyly was at the back of the show in the shadows of his own house. It would have been simple for someone to come up behind him, stab him, and slip away."

"Given that *everyone* was outside, any footsteps aren't conclusive of anything."

"There aren't any footprints anyway," Jack told him. "Greyly was standing on a stone path. He fell backwards or was pulled backwards. It was possible to kill him from behind and get away relatively clean. Especially if you knew what to expect."

BETH BYERS

Jack recapped what he'd found so far concerning Greyly, and Violet listened to her love speak. Jack's voice was a little deeper, a little husky, a little distracted. He was, she thought, rather like herself after they'd gone home. She'd been near useless because of her bad dreams. She thought that Jack might come away from the poor murdered mother and orphaned children with his own nightmares.

"Ham," Violet said. "The last case is wearing on Jack."

Hamilton Barnes winced. "That was a rough one. It has been weighing on my thoughts as well."

"We need to wrap this case up, and then you need to give him a break. I know he gets pulled in on the harder cases, the ones that are more sensitive or less clear cut. Like that poor viciously murdered mother. It's not good for Jack's heart."

Hamilton examined Violet's face. They had become friends, the two of them. Violet felt that she would always care for Ham by his own right, and not because he was like a brother to Jack. Even still, Violet met Ham's gaze fiercely.

"You're protecting him," he said.

"That's what you do when you care about someone."

The comment had them all pausing and staring at each other. "What if it is as simple as that?" Hamilton asked. "What if the killer was protecting someone? The rest of this doesn't make sense. The Hephaestus idiocy. The ghosts and mediums. Perhaps..."

"Perhaps," Jack said, taking Violet's hand, "we are grasping at straws for a reason behind this killing that makes sense to us. Though I don't disagree with you. I—" He shrugged. "Just playing devil's advocate."

Violet looked down at their hands where they were tangled together and relished the sight of his fingers wrapped around hers. "If it is that, we need to know who they all love."

"Or what they all love," Hamilton added. "People love things sometimes as much as the living."

"You've talked to them the most, Violet. While I've been in here swimming through this nonsense."

Violet nodded, distracted. "The Lovegoods probably love each other. Uncle and nephew and working together." She tapped her lip. "I seriously doubt that Jones cares about being an archeologist anymore. He has a backup plan and has for a while. I think Greyly's murder simply expedites things for Jones, though maybe makes them a little more difficult."

"Wendell?" Jack asked.

Violet didn't want to answer that question. She had a pretty good feel for Denny's brother, and she had little doubt that Wendell loved Dr. Lands like a second father. She suspected that Dr. Lands loved Wendell like a son.

She hesitated long enough that Jack nodded.

"Like Jeremiah Allen and myself?" Jack asked, referring to the young man who had looked up to and followed in Jack's footsteps.

"Except their relationship is current and unencumbered by a broken engagement."

"We could be overlooking the obvious." Barnes sighed. "These men have all been attempting to find a treasure in the past. Maybe one of them did?"

CHAPTER FOURTEEN

"If there is a simple reason for someone to slaughter another person, it's money. Change that money to actual gold or jewels or such, and you may just have an unconquerable temptation."

Violet stood and paced the office, playing with her ring while Jack and Barnes discussed the merits of the most obvious theories. Violet had little doubt the investigators would continue to comb through the letters and papers from Greyly and maybe they'd have an eventual reason to narrow their focus down to something else.

She had seen Jack follow the trail of clues more than once. He would take note of anything out of place in all the evidence and suddenly what was small would become important. It was *why* he was so good at discovering killers. Violet had meddled in more than one case, but she followed the people angle. The things she knew about those who had died. Sometimes, she'd used her status as an earl's daughter or a woman of wealth to get people to talk to her.

When someone had been murdered in her father's home, Violet had somewhere to start because the servants were willing to talk to her. The biggest problem with that was these men weren't connected to the people here. Likeliest person to have been starting those fires was the archeologist who didn't have a cheating spouse or alert servant to give up clues.

These men weren't stupid either. Regardless of getting involved in Greyly's idiocy, they *were* men of education. They'd simply been bought.

"If we were on their dig sites," Violet suddenly announced, cutting into the conversation between Jack and Ham as they discussed a letter about finances, "there would be diggers or assistants or locals to tell us more. These men—they're not connected to anyone here. We're held back."

"That's why we need to know why they were upset."

"But we already know that. Greyly had bought them with his money and the chance to work in archeology. He was, however, moving his interest towards ghosts. He had brought them home to cut them loose. This was a well thought out crime, however," Violet told them. "No mess on the killer? Hundreds of possible killers and witnesses but not one? It was risky. Terrifyingly risky to go after Greyly when they did."

"You don't think it was a crime of the moment?" Ham asked. He was testing her, and she shot him a disapproving look.

"You don't passionately kill someone in the middle of a crowd. Not with one of the knives he was using to muddy the waters of their findings. This was planned."

"Unless the two were arguing about the knife and it got out of control," Barnes told her.

She nearly rolled her eyes. "Then someone would have heard something. There would have been yelling, accusations, gesturing. One of the guests would have seen."

Barnes glanced at Jack. Both of them were looking at Vi as if she were a prized pupil. It was a little condescending, but she loved Jack and even Ham, so she was going to let it go. They had understood each other and left her to find her way after.

Violet lifted her brow at Ham. "You don't think it was a crime of passion either. Greyly's been maddening for years. You aren't looking for why someone got fed up. You're looking for the final straw that pushed someone over the edge."

"What changed," Jack said, but it wasn't a question. It was an explanation of what he'd been seeking. "You're right. I think it was one of the men who worked for Greyly."

"And you're right," Ham added, "that no one had any reason to note what these men were doing. They don't have connections here to trip them up and they're too smart to talk. Each of them guesses it was one of the others, but none of them knows each other well enough to pinpoint who was finally pushed too far."

Violet fiddled with her ring. "Unless you go back to someone who might be protecting another. Or if it's a treasure, you're either going to have to find it or watch for someone who suddenly has more money, and get them when they reveal the change in circumstances."

"You want to set a trap?" Jack glanced at Hamilton and then they both took a seat near the desk, with Jack pulling Violet to his side. He wrapped an arm around her waist and sighed. "The weakest links are those who care about each other. No one saw anything. There are no fingerprints on the knife. Any of them could have physically killed Greyly. We're looking for a needle in a stack of needles, and they're all the same."

"We might lose this one," Ham said. "It's early days yet, and we might catch a break. It seems unlikely, however, that we will. I'm not an admirer of murderers, but this one was well executed."

Violet pulled away from Jack to pace.

"We need to break and go home," Jack said. "To come back to it tomorrow and see if our men finding anything for us in the meantime. I'll interview everyone who hasn't been yet. See if I can find anything." Jack pressed his finger to the space between his brows, and Violet had little doubt that his head was aching.

"Shall we take bets?" Ham said, to lighten the mood. "Jones and Lands will say they were watching the show. Wendell will admit he was looking for that article. The Lovegoods will alibi each other, and the fainter won't have any defense at all."

"It was dark," Violet agreed, nodding at Hamilton's rundown of what could have happened. "If I hadn't been standing directly next to Jack and touching him, he could have slipped away without me knowing. That's the problem. Denny and Lila felt certain Wendell was with them until he wasn't. It was dark, it was crowded, we were blinded by the torches and the fireworks, and no one had any reason or ability to see into the dark shadows by the house."

"Interview them," Hamilton said. "I'll put a man on them as they leave. We'll follow them and look for anything that might give us a break in the case."

Violet wanted to come up with some clever answer. The best they could do was play the men off of each other. She didn't think that would help.

She waited for Denny and Lila to join her. Jack ran a few questions past them, but all they could say was that they had no idea when Wendell had disappeared into the darkness.

Denny hesitated as a maid brought Violet's coat, and Jack helped her into it. Then Denny said, "My brother is a good kid, Jack. He wouldn't have killed this Greyly fellow. Not even if he realized how badly his career could be ruined."

A part of Violet wanted to wrap Denny up in a hug and a part of her wanted to point out that he'd hadn't seemed to know that his brother was jealous. She stopped herself when she realized that it was possible that Denny *had* known. How did a lazy man deal with something like that? Let it go? Eat some more chocolates? Wait for it to blow over?

Vi would have asked Lila, but when she looked at Lila, she realized that Lila knew *exactly* how Denny felt and what he'd been doing to deal with the issues around his brother.

"How long has Wendell looked down on Denny?" Violet asked Lila.

Her friend winced as she took Denny's arm and hugged it.

"Hey now," Denny mused. "No need to see the worst in the blighter. He's young yet."

Lila shot Denny an exasperated look. "Wendell was always a bit of a well-meaning know-it-all who believed in hard work and good deeds to win the day. He never did like it when things went well for Denny if there didn't seem to be the corresponding hard work."

"He'll learn." Denny's look at his wife was so love-filled Violet had to hide her shock.

It wasn't that she hadn't believed Denny had loved Lila. Vi had known he did. She supposed she'd just assumed that Denny's laziness kept him from feeling emotions that deeply. Vi felt utterly repentant. She really should apologize to Denny at a later day. Perhaps with a box of his favourite chocolates and a bottle of his favourite drink.

"He's idealistic," Denny told Ham and Jack. "Wendell is *too* idealistic to commit murder. He didn't do it."

"I'll do my best to prove that," Jack said.

Denny hesitated and then nodded, holding out his hand. "I can't expect anything else."

They all knew what Jack hadn't said. He hadn't said he'd somehow let the murderer go if it turned out to be Denny's little brother. Wendell was in good hands, but they weren't forgiving hands. If Wendell had committed a murder? No one, not even Denny, would give the younger man a pass.

Violet rode back to Victor's house with Denny and Lila. They walked her up the steps and inside to find Victor sitting in the parlor, smoking a cigarette in the dark.

"Is Kate all right?" Violet asked.

Victor rose and walked quietly towards them, shooing them into the hall and shutting the door behind him. "She fell asleep on the Chesterfield waiting for you, Vi."

They turned towards the library and settled into seats around the room. They'd have requested tea, but they weren't quite that spoiled. The night was late, and instead they shared cigarettes as they caught Victor up on what had been discovered.

"There wasn't a great revelation?" her twin demanded.

"I wish there had been," Violet told them. "Jack is bothered by his last case. He doesn't have the energy for this one."

"Which is why he called in Barnes," Victor told her. "Don't worry about your love, Violet. Even he knows he's a bit off."

"Don't worry about your love," Violet told Victor. "It's normal for a woman to be sick while growing a baby."

Victor grunted. "Apologies, dear one, worry as you wish, and I'll do the same."

"Kate will be fine," Lila told Victor. She turned to Violet. "Jack will be fine. They're hardly alone. Unlike those archeologists of yours who don't have anyone to trip them up or connections to the rest of mankind, we're a family. We'll do whatever is necessary to get Jack back to being the best investigator around. We'll help take care of Kate, and all will be well."

Violet and Victor glanced at each other and then Victor said, "We'll help find your brother a better job *and* clear his name."

"Bit of a blighter really," Denny said around taking a long drag on his cigarette. He handed it to Lila, who had refused her own cigarette but was stealing drags off of Denny's.

"It's not like we don't have our own blighter brother," Violet told Denny. "We'll need you to commiserate when he gets out of school."

"Thought you were handling young Geoffrey," Denny said to the twins. He put up his feet and crossed them, glancing between the twins before he looked at his wife.

"We're losing that battle," Victor admitted and lit another cigarette. "The boy's a wart."

"Can't save them all," Lila told them.

It wasn't an answer any of them wanted.

"We're not done trying yet," Violet countered. "For Geoffrey or Wendell."

"All for one and one for all and all that," Denny added, stubbing out his cigarette and standing to pull his wife up. "It's late, love. Shall we conquer the world tomorrow?"

"After we sleep in," she said.

"And a good full English," he added. "Nothing chases a murder so well as eggs, sausages, roasted tomatoes, and beans."

Violet stood herself. Perhaps an answer would come in the morning.

CHAPTER FIFTEEN

*T*he dreams got her again. The one that made Violet want to crawl out of her own skin wasn't about Greyly and his dead eyes. That was the dream she had expected and been prepared to handle. Instead, she dreamed of the mother who had been killed and left behind her children. Somehow the dream twisted, so the dead woman from Jack's recent case was Violet's own mother, who had also died but not from murder, and Violet herself. At times, in the dream, it was even Kate. Except when the killer was coming for Kate, the baby was also at risk.

Violet tried to save each of them. Over and over again. She tried to stop the killer, but instead she lost them every time. Every time, she was too slow. Every time, Violet felt their blood on her hands, a feeling she had experienced before and never wanted to feel again. The worst part was, however, the baby. Her sweet Violet Junior. In the dream, the baby was a boy, and Violet had been nuzzling his nose with hers when the killer came from behind the shadows. The baby was killed and when Violet looked to the side, she saw Kate's eyes, staring and dead.

Violet's gasp turned into a whimper, and she pushed her eye mask back. The last thing she wanted was darkness. What she wanted was to curl onto her side and find Jack there, able to hold her to chase the dream away. She wondered if, across London, Jack was waking from his own dream about the murdered mother. He had been haunted and more human than he usually was since he'd come back from this last case. Before, he'd always kept his emotions in tight control, unless it pertained to her safety.

Usually, when Violet thought of Jack, she thought of this mountain of a man who loved her. In a world where she'd lost brothers to the war and seen more than her fair share of people die, he had always seemed like he could shield her with those broad shoulders of his. She felt safe when Jack was around. That hadn't changed. What had changed was that the lioness heart that she kept hidden behind merry jokes and light-hearted banter was ready to flex her claws and protect her love.

Violet rose and got her journal and a pen and then returned to her bed. She stacked her pillows high and deep to support her back and then crawled under the covers, propping her journal on her knees.

She wrote: SUSPECTS.

Violet had to admit she was a bit inured to murder victims, which she hated. Violet didn't care so much *who* killed Greyly. The most she could say was that she very much hoped that it wasn't Denny's brother Wendell. What Violet cared about was the darkness in Jack's gaze. The way he was distracted by the shadows in his thoughts.

She wrote out the names:

WENDELL LANCASTER

DR. STEPHEN LANDS

DR. SIMON JONES

DR. RICHARD LOVEGOOD—the uncle.

DR. LOVEGOOD—the nephew.

MR. LYLE CLARKSON

Violet focused on the only name she cared all that much about. She wasn't sure what to think of Wendell Lancaster. He was Denny's brother and opposite. Violet wanted to shake the man and tell him to appreciate Denny for who and what he was, but she also could remember her sister, Isolde, assuming that Violet wasn't on her side.

The problem with siblings was that relationships were complicated and these were wound up in the expectations and failings of a parent as well. Siblings might have been all right if they didn't hear their parents bemoaning a child. Or, if they didn't see the failure of a child and then how it affected the other people they loved.

Violet could imagine how seeing Denny fall easily into love and then easily into an inheritance while knowing exactly how hard Denny *didn't* work would be maddening for the child who *did* work and try.

And yet, Violet knew how great Denny was. She could remember when their friend Tomas was in the heart of his shell-shock and Denny—who hated to move—walked with him daily until Tomas had left London. Violet, herself, had asked Denny and Lila to help with orphaned children entirely unrelated to them, and they had opened their home without a second thought. Those children would be arriving that day, and Violet knew that the murder would pull her away from helping with them as she had promised, and yet she also knew that Lila and Denny would expect nothing else than for Violet to help find the killer and look after Jack.

The realization of how blessed Violet was to have Lila and Denny made her want to shake Wendell until sense filtered through his brain. She was angry when she filled out the notes after Wendell's name, and she knew it.

WENDELL LANCASTER— Motive? Certainly. He was caught searching through the Greyly's things twice. Wendell also had gotten what he thought was a dream job only to learn that the chance to work on a dig would ruin his reputation. This was made worse by having Greyly stop the digs he was supporting. Did his archeologists know that Greyly was moving on? Wendell wrote or put his name to Greyly's ridiculous article about Hephaestus. Did it have something to do with protecting his mentor?

Why, Violet thought, wondering the reasoning behind Greyly pushing that obsidian blade and volcano god madness. It was difficult to believe that a man who had been so capable of creating an empire with his finances would genuinely believe in something so ridiculous.

She would *love* to ask him about it. She was a business person who spent too many mornings reading reports and doing research on her own investments. She might have considered investing in some venture Greyly was behind until she found out about the madness of his theories. How many times had he ruined a business project because of his obsession?

Did Wendell realize that he'd been sucked into ruining his reputation for a man who wouldn't even keep him digging? At least for the other archeologists who had worked for Greyly, they had years of doing a job that was coveted even with the Greyly nonsense to go along with it.

Violet examined the next name and started filling in the information.

DR. STEPHEN LANDS—Motive? Not so sure about having a motive, given that he had worked for Greyly for years and knew what the man was. Would he have murdered Greyly if he knew that the dig was coming to an end? Was he getting vengeance for ruining his reputation? Something beyond the book he had been writing? Parker said Lands wouldn't get another dig after working for Greyly, and Lands didn't seem to have the money to finance his own operation. Did he have an alternate plan for his life? Where had he been during the fireworks show?

DR. SIMON JONES—Motive? Not sure about a motive. He seemed to have a plan in place. He knew what he wanted to do. He knew that his reputation was ruined as far as archeology went, but he didn't seem to be haunted by the idea. Where had he been during the fireworks show?

DR. RICHARD LOVEGOOD— Motive?

Violet sighed and looked up from her journal. Things seemed to be the same for both of the Lovegoods. They would probably alibi each other. Nothing appeared to have changed for them. Would they kill Greyly together? If one of them did it, would the other cover for him? It was hard to say. No one knew them well.

MR. LYLE CLARKSON — Motive? Money. Greyly's heir. He'd fainted when someone had inferred he had a reason to kill his uncle. He was the man's assistant, so if Greyly had been up to something nefarious, Clarkson might know better than anyone else.

Violet assumed that Jack would be tracking Clarkson down early today. As soon as it was reasonable to approach the man and discuss the murder with him, Jack would be at that door. She glanced at the clock on the mantle and saw it wasn't yet 7:00 a.m. She was tired all the way to her bones after the restless night and the dreams. Thinking back gave her the shivers, and she stared down at her useless journal. All she'd done was collect her thoughts, but she hadn't come to any conclusion regarding the murder, nor did she have any further thoughts on *why* Greyly had been killed.

In Violet's opinion, they all had motives. The question was why they were killing him after all this time. The only one who seemed to fall into the category of a recent reason to kill Greyly was Wendell. Violet wasn't going to go there in her head. If Wendell had killed Greyly, Violet didn't want to know about it, and she didn't want to see the effect of it on her friend.

She flipped through the pages and the recollection of what she'd discovered about her melancholy struck her again. On the days she was more active, she was less inclined towards the blues. Violet pushed her covers back and changed into her active clothes. She made her way to Victor's ballroom where they had their jiu-jitsu lessons, and Violet went through the motions she'd learned until she was sweaty and her legs were shaking.

If she needed to move to find a brighter outlook, then that was what she was going to do. Especially on the days when Jack was struggling to find peace as well. She started a bath for herself and added in some lavender oil and some Epsom salts and then sank into the water. How long until Beatrice returned with the children? Violet guessed it would be that very day. She would have to ensure that Lila and Denny had everything they needed for the children, that the man of business was pursuing the house on Victor's street, and that Jack knew that they were there to help however they could.

Violet slipped on her kimono when she got out of the bath and wrote notes for Jack, Jack's man of business, and Lila and Denny. The only one that really mattered was to Jack:

Darling Jack,

I've written to your man about the house as well as to my own. Focus on the case with the surety that we'll be escaping to the Amalfi coast as soon as we're free of this crime. Come for lunch if you can.

With all my love,

V-

Violet rang the bell and sent one of Victor's servants to hand deliver the messages. Then she examined her closet. She flipped through her dresses, noting how many Beatrice hadn't presented to Violet in the last few weeks. The maid had been dressing Violet to her own preference, Vi saw. She grinned at the idea and took one of the rarely-worn dresses. It was grey with a wide square neck, a dropped waist, and pleats that reached to her mid-calf. With the rainy day, the grey dress seemed just the thing. Violet counteracted the dullness of the dress and wool stockings with a cameo at her neck, golden earbobs, a light layer of powder, and red lipstick. With darkened lashes and penciled in brows, Violet's makeup was complete. She pursed her lips and grinned into the mirror.

Everything was brighter with red lips.

CHAPTER SIXTEEN

The breakfast room had been invaded by Mrs. Lancaster. Neither Victor nor Kate had arrived for the meal, but Violet faced the woman across the table.

"Where is my daughter?"

"Sicking up," Violet said, as she poured herself a cup of Turkish coffee and a cup of tea. Excessive? Yes, but her night was affecting her. "Did you just get in?"

"I took the early train," Mrs. Lancaster replied. "I expected someone to be down."

"Hargreaves probably told Victor that you were here. I'm sure he'll be down soon."

"I'll go up," Mrs. Lancaster replied. "My daughter needs me."

Violet knew she was on edge because of her dream, which is the excuse she gave herself for what she said next. "She doesn't, however."

Mrs. Lancaster's attention snapped to Violet, who smiled as gently as possible. "Victor is seeing to her. You can be assured that he'll take gentle and careful care."

Mrs. Lancaster's gaze narrowed on Violet—looking very much like an angry version of Kate—and snapped, "Sometimes a daughter needs her mother."

Violet had too many responses to that and too many of them weren't kind. She took a long drink of her coffee and let the flavour hold in her mouth while she thought. "Mrs. Lancaster, may I be frank with you?"

The woman also sipped her coffee before nodding once.

"Kate adores you. Victor likes you. I like you. You're the type of mother I want to be."

Violet wasn't finished, and Mrs. Lancaster was well aware of it when she said, "Thank you."

Very gently, Violet said, "You're smothering them."

The woman blinked rapidly, and she cleared her throat, nodding once. "I'll go."

"No one wants you to leave," Violet told her. "We need you. Just not in the bedroom while Victor is holding Kate's hair back. They need to suffer together for the baby. Victor needs to know just how difficult it is to bring a baby into the world. It'll make him a better father and husband."

Mrs. Lancaster sniffed. "Well, I guess..."

It was because Violet had been gentle, she realized, that Mrs. Lancaster had been willing to listen.

"Save us?" Violet begged. She reached out. "We have such a problem, and we need you," Violet told Mrs. Lancaster about the previous night's murder and the murder Jack had come back from working on in the north, and about the children. "He couldn't leave them. I couldn't watch him worry. We sent for the children, and they're coming to Lila and Denny's because Kate is so ill. But, I'm not ready to be a mother."

Violet let her eyes well as she confessed, "I am struggling with melancholy that comes and goes. Jack is haunted by what happened to their mother. Kate is too sick to have a stranger's children in the house. But we can't just leave them!"

Mrs. Lancaster was holding Violet's hand now. "Of course you can't. Though I'm not sure Lila and Denny are the right choice."

"They aren't. Denny's brother is the most likely suspect in Jack's case. If Wendell gets arrested and taken in for this crime, Denny is going to need time to recover and Lila will focus on him. I know they seem like they're idiots, but they're devoted to each other."

Mrs. Lancaster squeezed Violet's hand. "We could bring them up to the orphanage I'm managing for you."

Violet hesitated, biting her lip and waiting.

"Or we could find them a home."

She looked up at Mrs. Lancaster and suggested softly, "You are struggling for purpose with Kate here."

Mrs. Lancaster stared at Violet. They were both intelligent women, so Mrs. Lancaster didn't need Violet to explain what she wanted. Instead she closed her eyes and considered.

"How many of them are there?"

"Four," Violet said. "We could see to them financially. Their clothes, their nannies, their education."

"I do need something to do. How shall I raise them?"

"Love them like you do Kate and teach them to expect a good start. The same type of beginning to their life you'd give a child you were the natural mother to."

"So as if they were my own?" Mrs. Lancaster asked. There was a light in her gaze that told Violet that her guess that Mrs. Lancaster was at a loss was correct. She needed someone to love. These children needed someone to love them. Money shouldn't be a factor. Not when Violet and Jack had so much of it.

Violet nodded.

"You were going to wait until I volunteered?"

"I hoped you'd step in and save us. Since we were being bluntly honest, I decided to just ask outright. You don't need to fall in the blues too, Mrs. Lancaster. It's a hard place to be."

The woman laughed and let go of Violet's hand to drink her tea. "You're a clever woman. You got exactly what you wanted for Jack and Victor today."

Violet smirked and then said honestly, "And what I wanted for *you*. We're family now, ma'am. We'll meddle with you, you'll meddle with us, we'll love each other, and occasionally we'll have to just tell each other what we need."

Mrs. Lancaster rose and picked up a plate. She turned to Violet and her voice cracked as she said, "I'll love these children for you, but Kate is still my baby. I need to be part of her life as well."

"Ma'am," Violet told her, meeting her gaze straight on. "Kate would never forgive me if I tried to manipulate you out of her life. She needs to gain her balance with her new husband separate from you, but she *does* need you. We all do. You know we're orphans, right? Mother us too, please."

Mrs. Lancaster's laugh was wet, and she loaded her plate with chocolate pastries and bacon. Violet followed suit, telling the woman about her theory of physically moving to help keep the blues away.

"Exercise seems like a good choice."

"It helped Tomas when he was struggling with his shellshock. Denny walked with him for miles and miles if needed."

"Denny always was a sweet boy. Good to his mother. A bit hard of hearing whenever you wanted him to do something he didn't want to do, but sweet about it all. When his mother got quite ill after she had Wendell, Denny was underfoot constantly, reading to her, getting her whatever she wanted."

Violet smiled and admitted, "Sometimes I forget that you're his aunt. It feels like he's more ours than yours."

Mrs. Lancaster laughed. "He does choose you and your brother, you know. He and Lila could spend their time at home, but they don't. They choose you and your brother instead. Victor is more of a brother to Denny than Wendell ever was. A bit judgmental that one, inclined to feel he was righteous in his actions because he worked so hard. Yet, if their mother got sick again? Denny would arrive the next day, and Wendell would have to be tracked down."

Violet's brows lifted, and she told Mrs. Lancaster about Wendell's upset over the inheritance. His aunt wasn't surprised at either Wendell's feelings or Denny's surprise at those feelings. "Denny has always been a good boy. I hate to think that Wendell might have killed someone. His mother would go into hysterics at the sheer idea, but it is easier to believe it of Wendell than Denny."

Violet rose and started to pace the breakfast room until Victor arrived. "I'm so sorry ma'am," he said as he came into the room. "I should have come down as soon as you arrived."

"Nonsense," Mrs. Lancaster said. "Violet and I have had a good chat, and she's enlisted my help. Your job is to take care of Kate."

Victor's jaw dropped. A moment later he tried and failed to hide his reaction.

"I was smothering you. I knew it. Don't think you're getting rid of me because you aren't. You need to get your nursery in order, and not just for my grandchildren. These children will visit with me when I come, and I'll be coming often."

Victor turned to Violet, shocked. She winked at him and then shot him a look that told him to keep his mouth shut and agree to the demands. He did in a dazed sort of madness that needed him seated with Violet handing him a loaded breakfast plate and Mrs. Lancaster handing him a coffee. His mother-in-law left to look in on her daughter before she made a list for the servants regarding Victor's long-neglected nursery.

"Vi—" Victor blinked madly at his twin. "What in the world?"

"Mrs. Lancaster has agreed to save some orphaned children."

"What?"

"Kate is getting four adopted siblings."

"What?"

"Mrs. Lancaster is going to evolve from a smothering mother-in-law to a wonderful mother-in-law whose life is concerned with raising the poor orphaned children of a murdered woman while also being an attentive and caring grandmother."

"I—" Victor dazedly drank half of his coffee and then blinked at Violet as though ensuring she weren't a phantom. "Say that again."

Violet explained in detail. When she finished she said, "You now owe me forever."

He nodded blindly. "I do."

"You do," Violet repeated. "Don't worry. I'll remind you whenever it becomes pertinent."

Victor snorted into his coffee. "I have little doubt of that, Vi."

She grinned as someone knocked on the breakfast room door and then stepped inside. "My lady," Hargreaves said, "Mr. Wakefield's man of business has arrived."

Violet rose, squeezing Victor's shoulder as she left the breakfast room and joined the man in the parlor. "You received my note?"

"I did, my lady," he said. The man was an older fellow in a pinstriped suit with a bowler hat in his hands. "I also received a note from Mr. Wakefield."

Violet waved the man to a seat. "Were they conflicting?"

"Rather the same essential message, my lady, except yours requested that you pay half the amount for the house whereas Mr. Wakefield verified that he'd pay the entirety. I'll stop by the house and see what I can ascertain as to the sale of it."

Violet left the man to it, requesting that he come by Victor's house once the facts were acquired. She did not care if the money came from herself or Jack. They both had more than they needed and, in the end, it would be lumped together and given to their children.

Violet paced the parlor while she waited, until she finally got fed up with herself and went to the office that Victor had created for her. It was a smallish room near the library that held enough room for a desk and her typewriter. She'd had it lined with bookshelves and turned it into her own private writing and reading room.

She sat down in front of her typewriter and stared at the blank page for several long minutes before she started the story of an earnest young man, an archeological dig in Egypt, and the horrors that were found in the sand.

CHAPTER SEVENTEEN

*J*ack's man of business appeared at the same time as Jack, walking up the steps of Victor's house within steps of each other. When Violet was called to the parlor, Jack and Mr. Flannery rose in unison. Vi's gaze flicked between the two of them, but neither gave away whether they had been able to acquire the house.

"Well, Flannery," Jack said as they were seated again. "What have we learned?"

"They are moving," Flannery said. "They did intend to sell, and they are very interested in receiving an offer. The house is quite out of date though in good shape. I was able to examine it and even call in our firm's inspector. A new roof will be necessary before long. The floors need to be refinished. New paper. The furniture is intended to be sold with it, but I suspect you won't want to keep much of it. It's very worn."

"Did they accept the offer?"

"They are speaking with their man, but I think they will. I have little doubt that the house will be yours if you want it. The gardens are quite lovely. It's very roomy. Much larger than this house." The man laid out a sketch of the floor plan with detailed notes for every room. Violet glanced at Jack, who nodded, and she took them up.

"We'll do the repairs as soon as we can take possession," Jack told his man. "Make a list of everything that could possibly need to be fixed or updated. If we work hard and quickly, we should be able to have it done before the wedding."

Violet looked at Jack, certain that joy was shining in her eyes. She wouldn't have even dared to hope of a house so close to Victor's. One that she could redo. How much fun she would have replacing old furniture and having the place painted and papered to her specifications.

The man left with the notes he'd made, promising they'd be typed up and sent to her soon.

"We're buying a house without even seeing it," Vi whispered to Jack. "We must never tell Victor."

Jack laughed, and she saw how the darkness had faded from his gaze. Now to keep it out of him. "How did you sleep?" he asked, however, oblivious to her resolve.

She hesitated too long to get away with obfuscating the truth, so she admitted, "Not well. You?"

"The same," he replied.

"Did you find anything out today? Were you able to speak to Mr. Clarkson?"

"He took a rather heavy dose of sleeping pills and was unavailable when I arrived this morning," Jack said. "I told his man to make it clear I expected him awake and fully sober when I arrived after tea."

Violet tangled their fingers together, leaning her head on his shoulder. "Did you get my note?"

"I did," he said. "The Amalfi Coast will be just the thing. I will sleep in a chair overlooking the sea."

Violet played with her ring on her free hand and asked, "So what have you learned?"

Jack shook his head. "Greyly was a very odd man. Barnes found his journal this morning in the safe. The man had intended to use Hephaestus and the obsidian blades to give credence to a self-created cult."

"A what? Maybe they were the killers!"

"Except," Jack said, shaking his head, "the people who were part of it were together. It's in the interviews. They were interviewed separately, they all agree on their locations, and they have nothing to gain."

Violet leaned back onto his arm and muttered, "What fantastical nonsense."

"At least it explains *why* he was doing that weird archeological find with the obsidian blades. It wasn't for university acclaim, it was for this group of people."

Violet played with her ring as they sat together. "You have to wonder if the archeologists who were working for Greyly might have felt differently about their work if they had realized what Greyly was intending to do with it."

"I don't disagree with you there, but I talked to them last night, Vi. They know they're a laughing stock. The unfortunate part of this is the only one who wasn't fully aware of what he'd gotten into was Denny's brother."

Violet winced and then pushed up onto her knees next to Jack on the sofa. "Mrs. Lancaster has agreed to see to the children. She says she'll raise them, or at least give it a go."

Jack huffed out a relieved breath that Violet didn't think either of them had realized he was holding in. He cupped Violet's chin. "So this is what having a helpmeet is like. I tell you my worries and you solve them."

"Says the man who told his man of business to buy me a house today simply because it was two doors down from my brother's house, and to pay any price."

Jack leaned his forehead into Violet's, pressing them together. They shared the same air and a precious silence as relief filled them both. They relaxed into each other, curling towards one another as they breathed in and out in near unison. "I adore you, Violet Carlyle."

"I adore you, Jack Wakefield."

"April feels like it is forever away. Where shall we go on our honeymoon?"

Violet pulled a little back. "I'm not sure I really care where we go."

"I thought we might take a month somewhere warm."

"Somewhere with a blue sea?"

"And hot air."

"Cocktails with fruit?" Vi suggested.

"Hammocks in the sun."

"Sold on this idea, my good man," Violet said. The door to the parlor opened, and they turned to see Victor in the doorway. "I wondered how long it would take you to appear."

Victor winced, glancing over his shoulder and saying, "Perhaps some tea, Hargreaves." To Violet, he said, "Father can be more terrifying than you realize."

Violet snorted and propped her chin on her hand, with her elbow resting on Jack's shoulder, as she told Victor, "You are forever in my debt, twin."

"I won't be able to pay out, darling Vi, if Father kills me."

Violet twisted around, dropping back into a normal position on the sofa next to Jack. "Can you believe this cowardice?"

"Your father does have a way of promising you that he can kill you and hide your body forever in the same tone of asking if you'd like a cigar. I suspect you get your Machiavellian mind from your father."

Violet scoffed at both of them and then asked, "Where is Mrs. Lancaster?"

"She's gone to Denny's house," Victor answered, "to examine the nursery there and to meet Letty, who arrived this morning. Mrs. Lancaster says that Beatrice's cousin must meet with her approval before she takes up the role of full-time nanny for the children."

"Is Kate still ill?"

"She's sleeping off being sick," Victor said. "It wears her out, sicking up. She sleeps it off and then she's better for the rest of the afternoon."

"You should ask her mother if she ever discovered anything to help. Maybe there's some hedge witch remedy that will take the edge of it all off."

"She already gave me a list, and I sent Mr. Giles for it all. Ginger beer, tea, crackers, dry toast. I don't know. Some sort of tea mixture and herbs. I'm not sure. Ginger candies and peppermints."

Hargreaves arrived with the tea trolley, and behind him Hamilton Barnes entered.

"Did you get the house?" Barnes asked, as he slumped into an armchair. "We've had a break in the case, but I'm not heading back out without food and coffee."

"You heard the man, Hargreaves," Violet grinned. "Save him. Perhaps a platter of sandwiches and some coffee as well."

"Of course, my lady," Hargreaves said, leaving the parlor silently.

"What's the break?" Jack asked.

"We've caught Jones trying to sell some things he took from Greyly's house."

"He was stealing?" Violet demanded in awe. "And he got caught because of his tail?"

Barnes nodded. "Feel almost bad for him. He wouldn't have been caught without the shadow. We need to go down and question him. See if we can pin him down. Perhaps Greyly caught him taking things, and Jones killed the man."

"But there would have been a fight," Violet said. "The only way this murder would have worked without witnesses is if it was utterly quiet. Otherwise, people might have noticed."

"She's not wrong," Jack said.

Victor cleared his throat. "Wendell is still your main suspect, isn't he?"

The two investigators shared a look, and then Jack nodded once. Victor cursed and Violet poured them all tea as though a good cuppa could somehow change the fact that it was all too likely that Denny's little brother had killed someone.

"You could see how he'd have been so upset." Violet stood to pace after handing everyone a cup of tea. "He seems to be obsessed with working hard. If he realized that all his hard work was gone to the wayside, especially if he realized what Greyly wanted to do with the information he had these men plant, he might have snapped."

Jack explained Greyly's cult plan to Victor, who cursed again and then said, "I'm going to need some whiskey in my tea after hearing that nonsense."

Violet didn't want to spend her afternoon thinking about murder. She was so *tired* of it. She was tired of wondering why someone killed another person. She had seen enough of murder to be grateful that Ham and Jack did what they did. Murderers needed to be caught and punished so there would be less. Violet, however, wanted to go shopping for furniture for her house and start imagining her next bedroom.

"Did you discover anything else about the suspects?" she asked. "If you started with the assumption that Wendell was innocent, how would you proceed?"

Ham shook his head and rose as Hargreaves came into the room with a tray of sandwiches. He filled a plate with a stack and sat back down, leaving Violet's question to Jack.

"We can't do that, Vi. We have to follow the evidence. Right now, the evidence points to Wendell Lancaster, as painful as that might be for our friend."

Violet paced the room while they ate, wishing there were a way to discover the killer. She just couldn't allow herself to imagine Wendell as the killer. Not when she knew it would hurt Denny. Vi hadn't realized how protective she was of Lila and Denny until she'd seen them react to Wendell's vitriol, and she hadn't realized how much she respected Denny's heart until she'd seen him defend his brother after that nonsense.

If it were young Geoffrey? Violet considered her little brother and knew that she probably wouldn't be as kind to her brother as Denny was being to his. She hadn't expected to come to the conclusion that Denny was kinder than Violet was, but she was starting to suspect that it was the case.

She was as nearly surprised to discover that it wasn't all that shocking after she'd mulled the idea over. The question after that was—if Denny was right about his brother—how could she prove it?

CHAPTER EIGHTEEN

"*M*ay I come with you to question Jones?"

Hamilton winced and eyed Jack, who said, "Vi—"

She nodded. It was understandable. She wasn't an investigator, and Jones was at the Yard, not at some house party she had been attending. She continued pacing as Jack and Hamilton prepared to leave.

"Are you all right, Vi?" Jack had crossed to her and she glanced up at him and smiled.

"I'm fine, darling."

"I'll tell you what we find out."

He shouldn't be doing that either, but she wasn't going to argue with him about bending the rules for her. Instead she tilted her head and said, "I may just spend the afternoon shopping for possible house furnishings. Do you have any requests for colors?"

Jack grinned at her, and his eyes glinted. "You're excited."

"I am," Violet admitted. She tangled their fingers together and ignored Victor and Ham to press a kiss on Jack's cheek. "It'll be all ours. I think I'm happier that things need to be replaced than if it were all fresh."

"Perhaps not a very feminine master bedroom."

"Perhaps I can comply with that." Violet pressed a second kiss on Jack's cheek. "Gentlemen. Catch Jones as the killer, please."

She left them in the parlor and ran up the stairs to her bedroom to get her handbag, her coat, and to ring up Lila, who agreed to abandon Mrs. Lancaster to the children and come shopping with Violet.

"Do you think that Wendell is innocent?" Violet examined the Chesterfield in front of her. She could order one for her new home, but she wanted to see the house first. She simply wanted an idea of what was available. Her mind wasn't, however, on the Chesterfield or the armchairs she'd seen. Her mind was on the murder of Greyly. Violet told Lila about the cult of Hephaestus that Greyly had been trying to set up, and Lila had laughed until she cried.

"The stupidest part of it is that anyone who wanted to join his little bacchanal club wouldn't care if it were real or not. They aren't looking to justify what they're up to. It's a modern world where we don't have to remain imprisoned to the patterns of our ancestors."

Violet didn't disagree with Lila, even though it all struck Vi as utter nonsense. She followed Lila through the warehouse and asked again, "But you really don't think it was Wendell?"

"He's the most obvious choice?"

Violet nodded with a wince.

"I still don't think it was him."

"But—"

"Look, Vi," Lila said, stopping to face Violet. "I know where the evidence is pointing, and I understand why you think it might be Wendell. I swear to you that in my heart of hearts—I do not believe that it was Wendell. I do not believe that Wendell would, under any circumstances, kill someone. Please know, Vi"—Lila took Violet's hands, ensuring their gazes met—"I am *furious* with Wendell's attitude about Denny's inheritance."

"Then I don't think it was him either. How are we going to catch who it was?"

Lila shook her head. Violet felt a bit helpless. She wanted to save Wendell for them, but she had no idea how to make that happen.

She returned home after saying goodbye to Lila, both having lost joy in the purchasing of things for her house, and found Mr. Lyle Clarkson sitting with Victor.

"I thought I was supposed to meet Mr. Wakefield," Clarkson told them a little stupidly. Violet glanced at Victor, who shrugged.

"Did you send for Jack?"

Victor nodded, shooting Clarkson another look.

"Excuse us for a moment, Mr. Clarkson," Violet told him. She and her twin went into the hall. "What in the world?"

"I don't know," Victor said. "He knew where we lived from Greyly. As an assistant, he had the information from when Greyly visited."

"Is he really this idiotic?" Violet hissed.

"I think so," Victor admitted.

"Where is Kate?"

"She joined her mother at Denny's house to meet the children."

Vi winced. Lila probably shouldn't have left when she had. Though, Lila had gotten into the black cab with the explanation that she needed to escape the baby before she decided that it was time to have one of her own.

"What do we do?" Violet asked Victor. She knew what she *wanted* to do, she wanted to go in there and pin the murder on Clarkson instead of Wendell. "If he's really this simple, he can't possibly be the killer, can he?"

"I doubt it," Victor agreed. "Could he really be this simple or is it an act to hide the murder he committed?"

"Oh, that was a good point," Violet replied. She glanced back at the parlor. "Jack is going to need to do the questioning. Were you able to reach him?"

Victor nodded.

"We had better send for tea or coffee," Violet suggested, "and stop leaving him unattended."

They returned to the parlor as awkward as puppets with one string cut. Violet cleared her throat. "So, Mr. Clarkson, are you also an archeology enthusiast?"

Mr. Clarkson shook his head. "No, no. I—"

Violet told herself to not ask questions Jack would need the answer to, so she said, "Dreary weather we're having."

"Indeed, indeed." Clarkson glanced around the room and fell silent.

Violet shot Victor a look to take his turn at getting the conversation going. "You a fan of jazz, Clarkson?"

"No."

Victor glanced at Violet, who shook her head slightly, but he stared even harder. Her gaze narrowed on him and then she asked, "Do you care to travel, Mr. Clarkson? Victor and I were just discussing a trip to somewhere new."

Clarkson shook his head. "I prefer my own bed. Not one to gallivant about and waste money sleeping in someone else's bed."

Violet barely kept back the sound of an irritated scoff as she glared at her brother, a demand to take up his part.

"Ah, what do you enjoy?" Victor asked, as they all looked up in sheer relief as the tea trolley was brought in.

"I collect stamps and rare books."

"Oh, how nice. Victor and I enjoy books as well. What kind of books do you collect?"

"Religious treatises," Clarkson said.

Violet bit the inside of her mouth to hold back another frustrated grunt but then smiled prettily as she asked, "How do you take your tea, Mr. Clarkson?"

"Milk, four sugars," he said.

Vi grinned at the answer and made him a milky, sweet tea, handing the teacup and saucer to him. She made a cup of tea for her brother. He was a lemon-only man, and Violet poured a teacup for herself.

They drank the tea silently and when Jack arrived, Victor didn't even try to quiet the, "Oh thank goodness!"

Victor rose and crossed to Jack, shaking his hand and leaning in to whisper to him. Violet was sure it was a comment about Clarkson. She pasted a smile on her face as she poured Jack a cup of tea. She'd have added whiskey to it if Clarkson wouldn't have reason to make a fuss about it. She handed Jack the tea, and he grinned at her and took a sip before turning to Clarkson.

"Surprising to find you here," Jack said.

"You told my man that you expected to speak to me today. He —" Clarkson glanced about quickly and then timidly said, "He said you were quite upset. I wasn't sure where to go except for here. Uncle said you were engaged to Lady Violet."

Jack paused, blinking. "I did."

"Here I am," Clarkson said.

Violet bit her lip to hide a reaction and then hid it further behind her teacup. Jack cleared his throat. "Yes, well. You are your uncle's heir?"

"I expect so. There isn't anyone else really."

"But you aren't certain?" Jack frowned.

"He liked to say I was too stupid to have money. Wouldn't be all that surprised if it's all tied up and I just get a place to live and an allowance."

Violet bit down again on the inside of her mouth, this time to hide her frustration. Clarkson was the best bet for motive outside of Wendell. Clarkson smiled at Jack, a jolly expression, and said, "It'll be nice to not have my uncle around."

Vi pressed her lips together, not even bothering to hide her reactions.

"Oh?" Jack set down his teacup and pulled out his pencil and notebook. "Why is that?"

"He yells a lot," Clarkson announced.

Violet set her own teacup down, leaning back and closing her eyes. Her hopes for Wendell Lancaster to be saved by Clarkson's guilt were fading. There was something wrong with the way this man's brain functioned. Violet had to move Greyly out of the despised part of her mind, given that he had been allowing his nephew to work and his caring for the man.

She glanced at Jack, searching his face to see if Jack thought it was an act, but she didn't think he was doubting Clarkson. Violet played with the ring on her finger, rising to pace the parlor while Jack asked Clarkson more questions. By the end of the interview, it was apparent that Clarkson actually had an alibi the whole time. He'd been helping the people who had been setting off the fireworks. Violet knew Jack would double check, but she didn't doubt it was legitimate.

"Back to Wendell?" Violet asked as Clarkson left the house. "Or did you learn something from Jones?"

"Nothing you'll like," Jack told her. He set aside his notebook and propped up his feet. "Jones didn't alibi the Lovegoods because he was thieving, but he saw them during the fireworks show. He's certain that they were together and that they didn't kill Greyly. Jones was taking things from the ballroom, which was unattended. The Lovegoods were smoking near the back of the crowd. He also said that they let Greyly support their digs, but they could afford to dig on their own. Greyly's death won't ruin them in the same way it'll ruin Lands, Wendell, and Jones's own dig."

"Damn it!" Violet let the worry for Wendell fill her face.

"I'm sorry, Violet. I do have an idea, but it requires Hamilton's approval since it's out-of-bounds of normal Yard procedure. It also requires Wendell to go along with it."

Violet's brows lifted, and she leaned forward.

"Tell me."

CHAPTER NINETEEN

"*D*id you find anything out from Jones that would change things for Wendell?"

Jack shook his head.

"You think this is going to work?"

Jack shook his head, but he tangled his fingers with Violet's. "But we'll try."

"For Denny," Violet said.

"This is completely irregular," Hamilton said. "It's just as easy that Wendell and Dr. Lands were working together."

Violet patted Hamilton on the back. "You're a good man, Ham."

"I'm not sure how I let you talk me into this," Hamilton told Jack, giving him an exasperated look.

"It's the villa on the Amalfi Coast," Violet told him. "You have time off coming up, and you want to go with us. We can't go if this case is lingering on."

Hamilton snorted. "As though you wouldn't let me stay there

without you. Try again, Lady Violet. I know your generosity too well."

Violet laughed. He had her there, but he was as worried about Jack as Violet was. Even as they waited for Parker to appear with Dr. Lands, Jack was caught by the shadows again. Vi didn't know what had happened in the north, but she was certain she didn't *want* to know. She was already having bad dreams about whatever had happened without her knowing. Maybe her imagination was filling the blanks worse than it had been, but every time that thought struck her, she remembered the look in Jack's gaze and thought it was worse than even she was imagining.

She glanced at Hamilton, who looked as worried as Violet was about Jack. They were standing in the ballroom of Greyly's house where the displays had been half-emptied. "How did anyone not notice so many of these had been partially emptied, and where did Jones keep the contents?"

"We were focused on the body," Jack said dryly. He cupped the back of her head and pulled her close to him, pressing a kiss on the top of her head. "Let's get into position."

It was a stunt they'd pulled before. Getting the murderer to confess while they listened. Now it was up to Dr. Henry Parker to convince his old friend that he'd seen what had happened and trip up the man who had murdered his one-time patron flawlessly.

Violet followed Jack to the hall off of the ballroom while Hamilton took position on the other side of the room.

Jack tucked Violet close to him and then turned her so they were pressed against the wall in the hallway. If anyone walked down the hall towards them, they would only see his arm and possibly her skirts fluttering between his legs. If Dr. Lands decided to get violent, Violet would be safe. She laid her head against his chest and listened to his heart for long, silent minutes.

Eventually there was a clatter in the ballroom followed by the sound of footsteps. Voices lowered in speech reached Violet and Jack, but at first the words were indistinct until the men reached the center of the ballroom.

Why were they talking about the weather? She shot Jack an exasperated look.

"They need a catalogue of all the items and then we'll value the things that Jones stole for his case. Shouldn't take too long." It was Parker's voice. Violet pressed her face into Jack's neck as she listened, to muffle any sounds from her reactions.

The sound of the men opening the cases carried on for a while and then Parker asked, "When are you going to explain why you did it?"

There was a long pause that Violet desperately wanted to witness with her eyes instead of just her ears.

"Why would you say that?" Dr. Lands laughed, but it was a hollow thing.

"It's easy enough to figure out," Parker told him. "Even if I hadn't seen you stepping away from the body. Jones didn't care enough to kill Greyly and doesn't get anything out of his death. I'd have believed it of him if Greyly's expensive ring disappeared or that old ruby fob on his watch chain."

"So it was me?"

"We both know Clarkson is too dim to think of killing Greyly, and even if it occurred to him, he's too weak to follow through."

"What about the Lovegoods?" Lands demanded. "Why must you try to pin this on me?"

"I saw you, old man. I knew about your book, the things you documented. Why would you suddenly change your mind and kill Greyly? What possible benefit could there be for you?"

The silence was intense. *Had* Parker seen Dr. Lands? Violet hadn't believed so, and yet she was convinced he had after hearing him speak. As far as Vi knew, Parker was trying this because she'd promised that if he got a confession, she'd finance a dig in Egypt for five years, with Wendell as part of his dig. Perhaps Parker decided to go all in like some sort of American cowboys and bad guys' poker game?

Violet bit her bottom lip to hold back her questions and any tell-tale gasps. A choice that made her particularly grateful when she heard Dr. Lands say, "Why didn't you say anything to the police?"

Parker cleared his throat weakly before he answered, "I never liked Greyly, and I never liked how he ruined your career. We've been friends for a long time, Stephen. Long enough for me to wish a different fate for you many times over. I never—I...by Hades, man, *why?*"

Violet peeked through the crack in the door, daring to look and saw Dr. Lands slump into one of the chairs that had been brought in so they could appraise the collection.

"The boy, of course. It was like watching my life fall apart all over again as he realized what Greyly's scheme would do to his career. Poor Lancaster didn't see it at first."

"They think it was him," Parker told Lands. "Stephen, they think it was the boy."

"Over Clarkson? He has financial motive."

"You didn't account for Clarkson's idiocy," Parker told Dr. Lands. "You were too smart and too brave for anyone to believe the killer was Clarkson. No one who meets him and talks to him would think he would have the spine necessary to walk up to a man at the back of a crowd, shove a blade in at just the right spot for him to fall silent to the ground, and walk away as cool as you please."

Lands paused, looking up at Parker. "I—are you...are you setting me up?"

Parker flushed and shook his head. "Of course I'm not. Why would you?"

The two friends stared at each other and then Parker breathed out, "You cut his throat."

"Where are they?" Lands demanded. "Where—"

Lands shoved at Parker, knocking him to the ground, and ran for the French doors. Jack's protective bulk left her as he gave chase. Only a moment behind him was Hamilton Barnes.

Violet slowly walked into the ballroom. She had thought it must be Dr. Lands. Out of sheer process of elimination rather than anything else. It had been a near-perfect crime.

"He would have gotten away with it," Parker said from the ground. She offered to help him up, but he shook off her hand. "This was a dirty business. Yet I find I am concerned you won't pay those 30 pieces of silver."

Violet flinched, but she wasn't afraid of the truth. "The boy he was trying to protect would have gone to jail for his crime."

Parker straightened his tweed jacket and his glasses, smoothing his hand over his head. "He might have gotten off. There was no evidence to tie him to the crime."

"His life still would have been ruined. You know his family describes him as earnest and hardworking. Does he deserve to have his life destroyed because someone else committed murder?"

"For him," Parker shot back, but Violet could see his heart wasn't in it. He simply felt guilty for his part in rapping his friend.

"You'll get your silver," Violet told him, heading towards the front of the house. Jack and Hamilton couldn't take her home, but the servants who were left could call her a black cab. She could go home, curl up in her bed, and be grateful that there was no reason anyone would commit murder on her behalf.

It only occurred to her as the cab parked in front of Victor's house that she had more reasons to be grateful than that no one had a reason to kill on her behalf. She had little doubt there were a good handful of people who *would* kill to protect her. And, she told herself, there were even more who would mourn her. She sat in the black cab for too long, and eventually Hargreaves came down the steps, paid the man, and brought Violet inside.

She let him hand her up the stairs, and as they went, she asked, "How would you like to spend the rest of November in Italy?"

He opened the front door of her home. "I would like that, my lady."

Violet didn't immediately go inside the house. Instead, she turned to look down the street to the grey stone house on the corner with the large garden. In either house, she'd have a home because of the people who loved her. In either house, she'd have safety and security and peace. But she wouldn't have Hargreaves. She grinned up at him, winked, and asked, "How much of a raise will it take for you to abandon my lesser twin and run my house instead?"

"Hey now," Victor said, as he pulled Violet inside. "We will have to create some sort of schedule instead, and we will share him. Did Jack get his man?"

"He did."

"And it wasn't Denny's brother."

"Dr. Lands."

"Thank God," Lila said from a doorway. "Denny! It wasn't Wendell."

Violet followed Lila into the parlor were Denny had his head between his knees as he breathed slowly in and out. He finally sat up and asked, "How?"

Violet explained what had happened, and Denny stared for a long time before he spoke. "Why did they do that? If it didn't work—Dr. Lands would know they didn't have anything on him."

"He probably already knew that," Violet said. "They risked it because I promised Parker I would finance a dig."

"But why did *Jack* and *Hamilton* try it? It could have ruined their case."

Violet reached out and smacked Denny on the back of the head. "You're family, Denny. You were sure it wasn't Wendell, so they operated as though you were correct. If it wasn't Wendell, the only logical person who could have done it was Dr. Lands."

"So they tried this trap because they believed in me?"

Violet nodded.

"*Over* Wendell?"

Violet nodded and glanced to Lila, only to see her friend with tears in her eyes. Violet slowly turned her baffled gaze to Victor, whose head was tilted as he examined his friend.

"No one likes me or trusts *me* over Wendell, Violet." Denny sat up. "*No one.* Most people don't trust me at all."

Violet smacked the back of Denny's head again, but she took his hand and said clearly and precisely. "We do."

"You do?" Denny demanded, as though he couldn't believe her.

"We do," Violet said. "It's over. We've won. They've won. I don't know the right way to say it since we shouldn't have been involved at all. We're done with the case."

Victor closed his eyes in relief. "Time for a cocktail."

"With a side of chocolates," Denny declared.

"Indeed," Violet agreed. "Nothing else will do."

"I've been thinking on it," Jack said a week later, as they took a yacht out onto the sea. The blue ocean was shining below and the sky was bright and clear overhead. It wasn't warm given that it was November, but it was warmer than London.

"On what?"

"Our bedroom," Jack replied. "Grey and dark blue. Those are the colors I like."

"May I have dragons?"

Jack nodded.

"What else?"

"I should like a garden bench," he added. "For sunny days to read your books in the garden."

"That sounds lovely. I should like to sit with you on that bench and read other authors' books. What else do we need for it to be ours? Beyond the grey and blue bedroom and the garden bench?"

"I shall need to carry you over the threshold," Jack told her, pushing up on his elbow and tangling his fingers with hers. They were lying side by side on the deck chairs as the yacht moved over the water. Violet lay her head on his arm, letting the sound of the wind, the sea, and the gulls fill her.

"I like this dream," she said.

"It's not a dream." He turned her face to his and pressed a kiss on her forehead. Another kiss to her right cheek and then one to her left. Finally, he kissed her breathless before he pulled back, staring into her eyes. "This is our life."

"What a lovely life it is," she said, resting her head against his chest.

The END

Hullo, my friends, I have so much gratitude for you reading my books and enjoying them. Are there words enough to explain how that feels? Almost as wonderful are reviews, and indie folks, like myself, need them desperately! If you wouldn't mind, I would be so grateful for a review.

The sequel to this book, *Murder at the Ladies Club, is currently available.*

January 1925.

Violet Carlyle is in the midst of wedding preparations somehow balancing her stepmother's snobbery with her own wants. Since Lady Eleanor arrived in London, Vi's beloved Jack has thrown himself into case after case.

Out of sheer boredom, Violet accepts an invitation to attend the Piccadilly Ladies Club. When she makes some new friends at the club, Violet accepts an invitation for a party. She little expects to stumble over a body over an evening of cocktails and conversation. Together, Jack and Violet step into the investigation determined to discover why this woman was murdered and if anyone else is at risk.

Order Here.

I am delighted to announce the coming of a new historical mystery series, *The Poison Ink Mysteries* and the first book, *Death By the Book*.

Inspired by classic fiction and Miss Buncle's Book. Death by the Book questions what happens when you throw a murder into idyllic small town England.

July 1936

When Georgette Dorothy Marsh's dividends fall along with the banks, she decides to write a book. Her only hope is to bring her account out of overdraft and possibly buy some hens. The problem is that she has so little imagination she uses her neighbors for inspiration.

She little expects anyone to realize what she's done. So when *Chronicles of Harper's Bend* becomes a bestseller, her neighbors are questing to find out just who this "Joe Johns" is and punish him.

Things escalate beyond what anyone would imagine when one of her prominent characters turns up dead. It seems that the fictional end Georgette had written for the character spurred a real-life murder. Now to find the killer before it is discovered who the author is and she becomes the next victim.

Order Here.

If you want book updates, you could follow me on Facebook.

ALSO BY BETH BYERS

Cookies & Catastrophe

(found in the Christmas boxset, The Three Carols of Cozy Christmas Murder)

Poison & Pie

Double Mocha Murder

Cinnamon Rolls & Cyanide

Tea & Temptation

Donuts & Danger

Scones & Scandal

Lemonade & Loathing

Wedding Cake & Woe

Honeymoons & Honeydew

The Pumpkin Problem

The Brightwater Bay Mysteries

(co-written with Carolyn L. Dean and Angela Blackmoore)

A Little Taste of Murder

(found in the Christmas boxset, The Three Carols of Cozy Christmas Murder)

A Tiny Dash of Death

A Sweet Spoonful of Cyanide

ALSO BY AMANDA A. ALLEN

The Mystic Cove Mommy Mysteries

Bedtimes & Broomsticks

Runes & Roller Skates

Banshees and Babysitters

Hobgoblins and Homework

Christmas and Curses

Valentines & Valkyries

Infants & Incantations (Coming Soon)

The Rue Hallow Mysteries

Hallow Graves

Hungry Graves

Lonely Graves

Sisters and Graves

Yule Graves

Fated Graves

Ruby Graves

The Inept Witches Mysteries

(co-written with Auburn Seal)

Inconvenient Murder

Moonlight Murder

Bewitched Murder

Presidium Vignettes (with Rue Hallow)

Made in the USA
Middletown, DE
27 June 2019